I0686888

RESONTAS

J. B. DE BORD

Copyright © 2023 J.B. De Bord

This is a work of fiction. Names, characters, places, and incidents either are the product of the author's imagination or are used fictitiously. Any resemblance to actual persons, living or dead, events, or locales is entirely coincidental.

ISBN: 979-8-9897158-0-0

Design by J. B. De Bord
Cover by J. B. De Bord
Edited by P.J. Hoover

For Garsevan and Johnny. Two bright sparks.

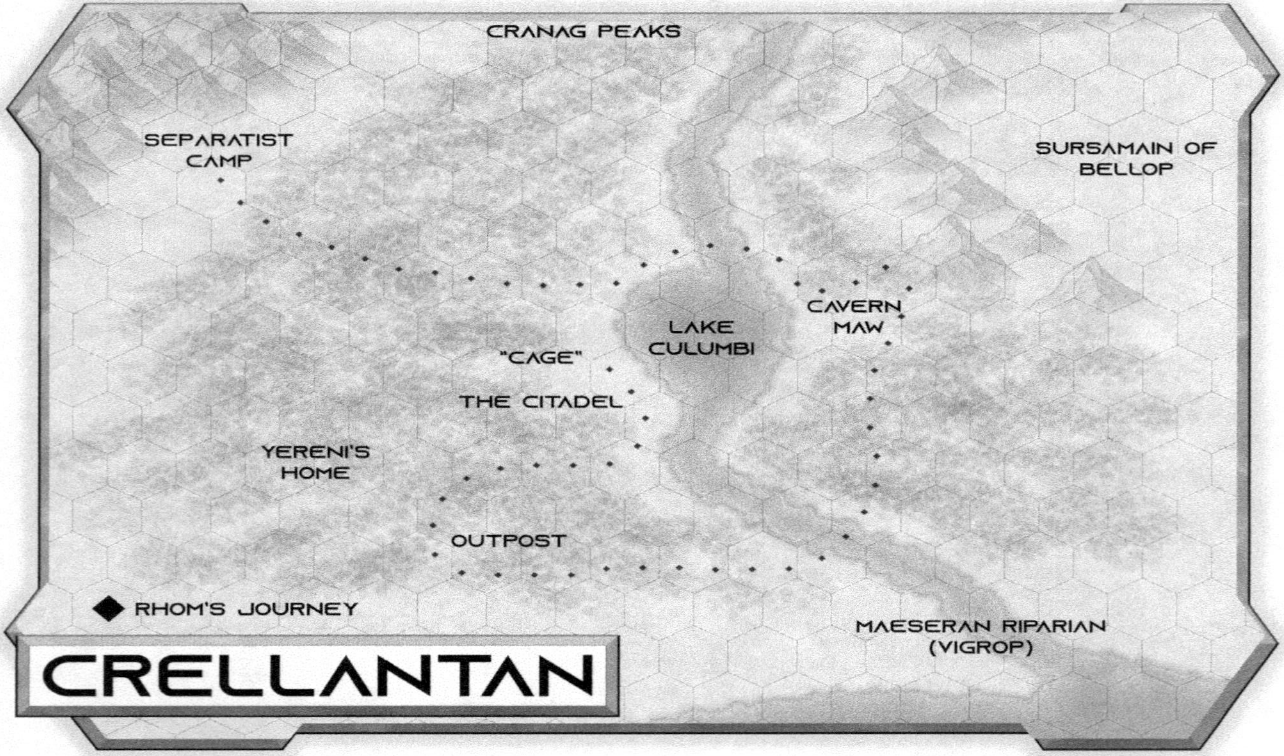

CRELLANTAN

◆ RHOM'S JOURNEY

SEPARATIST
CAMP

CRANAG PEAKS

YERENI'S
HOME

OUTPOST

THE CITADEL

"CAGE"

LAKE
COLUMBI

CAVERN
MAW

MAESERAN RIPARIAN
(VIGROP)

SURSAMAIN OF
BELLOP

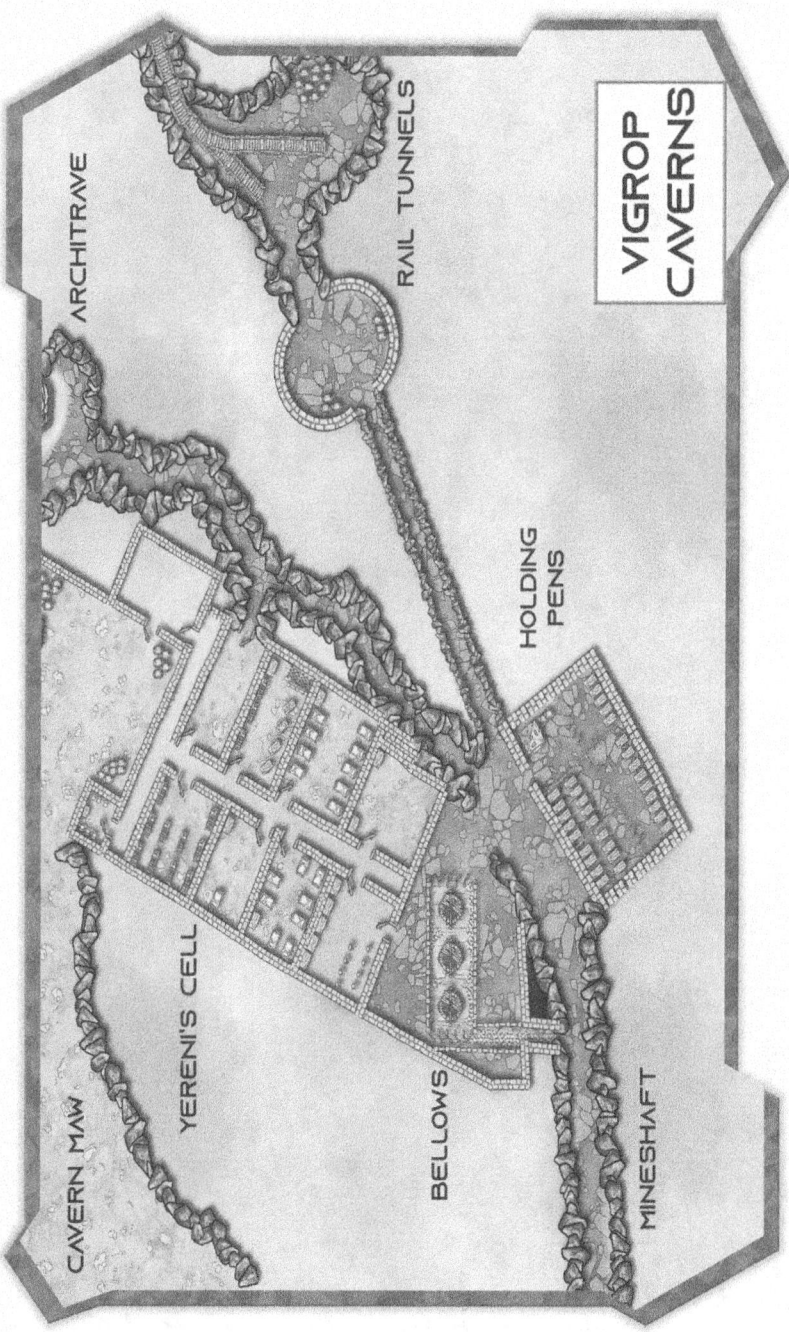

VIGROP CAVERNS

ARCHITRAVE

RAIL TUNNELS

HOLDING PENS

CAVERN MAW

YERENI'S CELL

BELLOWS

MINESHAFT

GLOSSARY

Ahkaiyee (ä-kī-yē): A former Keeper. He suffered from separation fever after trying to free himself from Visatae connection.

Bellop (bel-äp): Sentient simian of limited intelligence who live along the ridgeline east of the Havens. Constantly raiding the outskirts of the Havens. The Sursa is their king.

Bendohl (ben-dōl): Yereni's father. One of the original members of the Lab and part of the party who discovered the Visatae eggs.

Berendi (ber-en-dē): Jambat from the Northern Bellop/Crelli border fond of kamburi feathers. Light on his feet.

Berhpas (ber-päs): Advisor to the Separatist movement. Former acolyte to the Masari. Helps Rhom to discover Resontas.

Brawzen (brō-zen): A former Keeper. Uncle to Terth and surrogate father to Rhom.

Cloi (klō-ē): Niece of Old Raunt. One of the seven Stranded imbued with vespridium.

Cornas (kōr-näs): Forest beast. Has three tentacles covered in scales. A central mouth and stomach sack and a deadly barbed poison whip-like tongue

Craznak (kräz-nak): Jambat from the river region, wears turtle shells. Strong of body but not of mind.

Crellan (krel-än): The Crelli people, when referred to as a whole or as a culture.

Crellantan (krel-än-tän): The sum of all life as referred to by the Crelli.

Crelli (krel-ē): The singular or plural reference of an indigenous humanoid dwelling in the valley (I am Crelli, or we are Crelli.)

Crepus Caliginous (kri-pəs) (kə-li-jə-nəs): The misty twilight realm found on the other side of the Preternal Architrave.

Culumbi (kə -ləm-bē): The main body of water near the Crelli lands. Location of the first Visatae egg discovery.

Cycle: 8 Seasons

Delpar (del-pär): Jambat from the Havens, likes to trap creatures for amusement, not exactly trustworthy.

Garthag (gär-thag): Bellopian warrior of the Bellopian Dobai

Jambat: (jəm-bət) A Jamtori in training

Jamtori (jəm-tór-ē): Military extension of the Jaruvian religion. Selected and trained to operate in conjunction with the Visatae.

Jaru (jó-rü): Central figure of the Crelli religion. Jaru is understood to be the creator of life and the planet Crellantan.

Jaruvian (jó-rü-vī-ən) **Monk**: Spiritual guide of the religion of Jaru

Kallopod (kaló-päd): Slug like forest creature

Kamburi (kəm-búrē): A four-legged bird found in the hills just outside the valley near the Crelli/Bellop border to the north.

Kindal (kin-däl): Seven cycles or fifty-six seasons

Kindrel (kin-drəl): Seven symbols for the seven axioms of the Jamtori. Representing Courage, Honor, Benevolence, Loyalty, Truthfulness, Morality, and Duty.

Maeseran Riparian (mī-ser-ən) (rə-per-ē-ən): The lands occupied by the Vigrop.

Mallahen (ma-la-hen): Yereni's mother

Masari (mä-sär-ē): Head of the Crelli Poli-religious government and leader of the Jaruvian religion.

Moori (múr-ē): Shy Crelli from the lake side pods.

Preternal Architrave (prē-tər-nal) (är-kə-trāv): a doorway leading to the Crepus Caliginous

Radoacs (rad-ōks): Winged forest creatures who prey upon the near dead.

Raunt (ránt): A veteran Jamtori and head trainer at the Citadel.

Refulgenae (ri-fúl-jən-ā): Creators of the language of light and precursors to the Remplancant

Remplancant (rem-plan-känt): Imprisoned creator of the Visatae

Resontas (re-zən-təs): Clearing one's mind to access a higher level of spiritual being.

Rhomazel "Rhom" (räm-a-zəl): Orphan Crelli raised by Brawzen. One of the seven Stranded imbued with vespridium.

Sheidel (shī-dəl): Known for her agile and swift climbing abilities. Her favorite pastime before coming to the hatching had been chasing jindips across the treetops until finally catching one and petting its belly until it fell asleep.

Sherundi (she-rün-dē): Rhom's mother

Shives (shī-ves): Second in command to Worlz

Skelkiz (skel-kiz): Vigrop leader of the excavation site controlled by Berhpas.

Sloazian (slō-zē-ən): Tree dwelling creature with multi-jointed legs. Sometimes referred to as a Walker. Often cultivated for food.

Snifty (snif-tē): Small woodland creature

Splincer (splin-sər): Widowed Crelli neighbor of Rhom

Sursamain(sər-sa-mān): Lands of the Bellop Nation

Sylpah (sil-pē): Cloi's mother

Teleg (tel-eg): A former Keeper from the same group as Brawzen who lost his sight. Now a storyteller living in the Havens.

Terth (tərth): Best friend of Rhom and nephew to Brawzen. One of the seven Stranded imbued with vespridium.

Thaan (thän): Rhom's father

Vaetris (vī-trēs): Terth's mother

Valden (val-dān): Crelli Jambat from the Havens with expensive habits. Doesn't take well to being told no.

Vespridium (ves-pri-dē-əm): An unknown element discovered with the Visatae eggs. Crelli experiments with vespridium led to its common use as a power source.

Vigrop (vi-gräp): Lizard men from the forest edge southwest of the Havens

Visatae (vi-sə-tā): Insectoid creatures who bond with the Crelli mentally. The creation of the Remplancant.

Visatae Dobai (vi-sə-tā) (dō-bi): Winged Visatae warrior class.

Worlz (wór-əls): Leader of the Separatist soldiers. One of the seven Stranded imbued with vespridium.

Yereni (yer-ə-nē): Forest dwelling Crelli. Rescues Rhom from near death in the forest. One of the seven Stranded imbued with vespridium.

RESONTAS

J.B. DE BORD

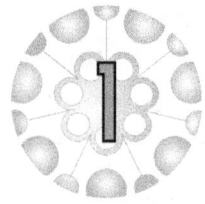

The midday sun reaching its apex arced across the hazy pink sky. Casual chirps, trills, and songs rang out among the leafy branches. Crellantan was a forest full of activity, spanning the eastern plateau lands of the dreaded Bellop to the razor-sharp cliffs west. Cool, clean water flowed from the northern falls into the great lake Culumbi before passing the dwellings of the Havens and onto the southern marshlands.

"C'mon Terth!" Rhom said. "We're gonna be late for the hatching." The two boys had been daydreaming again. "You know how uncle can be when we are late." Standing above Terth, the sun overhead created a hazy silhouette around Rhom.

"So go by yourself Rhom. I'm not done with my nap," Terth said with a sly grin.

It had been another morning of busy nothings and, as usual, their free time had raced by. Rhom stood and peered out from a leaf-covered platform. The forest canopy beamed a brilliant deep red with accents of pink, yellow, and orange. It was a sharp contrast to the dull, flat gray of the branches peeking out from the openings. Gazing across the valley, the colors faded to a hazy burgundy. Far north, the Cranag peaks stood aloof, blanketed in pink-tinted snow. This was the view from their private hangout near to the edge of the forest, west of their home village. The boys nicknamed this hangout "The Cage." It was an interwoven basket of tangled branches and leaves accessible only by leaping down from above.

They spent the greater part of their free time in and around the Cage. Most days, Terth would end up inventing some game of skill and challenge Rhom to beat him. In the early years, Rhom would try wholeheartedly, only to end up losing to Terth. These days he showed enough effort to make the win feel real. After winning, Terth would often goad Rhom with some kind of knee-capping remark.

Terth rolled over to his side and popped a berry into his mouth. Loudly chewing, he spoke, "We have plenty of time. There is no need to rush and waste this amazing morning. I know I won't be late, and you are the slow one, anyway. You see Rhom, that is why I will be head of the Jamtori, and you will end up picking berries with Splincer." Splincer happened to be their neighbor, a kind widow the boys thought was at least 300 cycles old.

"Ok, since you think you're the best, prove it by being there so they can choose you," Rhom said.

Terth sat up and made his way to the opening. Terth was slightly larger than Rhom with darker hair and sharper facial features. Climbing up and free from the bower, the two scanned the area. One more check before diving into the thick forest canopy. Leaping and swinging, they made their way across the trees east toward home.

The two had been together as long as they could remember. They were inseparable. Their families were some of the oldest in the valley. Uncle Brawzen often said they were the direct offspring of the founders of Crellantan. Those first awakened in the Emergence.

Terth stopped to adjust his gear. Both boys were wearing a gray leather harness over a light single-piece suit ending at the knees and elbows. The body suits were in woven patterns of variegated grays and dark reds, blending with the forest. Their short hair was encircled by a padded headband, a necessary protection from any impact by the many whipping branches. Rhom shouted out. "Let's go! We can't be late. I always get the blame when things go wrong. You say this is your year? Well, then race me to the Citadel."

Terth shot up several feet, making a tight somersault before grabbing the next branch with a grin. "You're on!" he said, and the two took off across the branches and through the forest.

The complex structures of the vibrant Crelli cultural center slowly came into view through the floating mists of the leafy canopy. sprawling away from the river toward the western side of the lake like the arms of a squid winding their way around the largest trees. The fresh water and abundant fertile soil between the northern lake and central outflowing river made the Havens ideal. Over time, the simple structures of the original inhabitants were replaced with improved materials. The Temple, Rookery, and Jamtori barracks were the only remnants of the original buildings.

As they drew near to the Havens and home, the noise of the crowd became louder. The smell of fresh roasted meats filled their nostrils. Sweet aromas of freshly picked fruit from vendors filled the air. The two friends turned the last corner to see the crowd gathered around the Rookery and the master himself, Old Raunt.

"The time is near. Find your sponsors and prepare

yourself," Old Raunt proclaimed from the open dais. The white walls of the Citadel grounds towered behind him.

His bellowing voice echoed off the walls. Old Raunt had been the head trainer at the Rookery since the great Bellop Wars with the tribes to the south. The scarred remnants of a large gash could still be seen leering out of the collar in Raunt's chest piece. Secured to the back of his harness was an odd blue-gray cannister. Raunt oversaw the Jambat progression into full Jamtori, the elite guardians of all Crellan.

The clearing, nicknamed the Commons, was full of Crelli engaged in last-minute transactions, conversations, and warm embraces of long-time friends. Behind the southern wall stood the ancient temple grounds, comprising a large central dome with spires on either side. Beyond the ancient main dome, newly constructed barracks and a connecting courtyard glistened. Buried deep below the east spire along the river the Crelli built the Rookery.

Any other day, marketers and vendors would occupy stalls along the northern end of the Commons, offering tribute to the Citadel for their use. Before the hatching ceremony, the stalls were emptied, cleaned, and prepared for the candidates vying for acceptance.

The Ceremony began the usual way, Raunt reciting the history of the Crelli. First, recounting the Emergence of the Crelli by the hand of the Goddess Jaru, followed by the Great Calamity that befell all. The story of land quakes throughout the valley resulting in a large sinkhole. Large masses of water had swelled and washed away portions of the Crellan homeland. Many lives were lost. The visual proof lay in the great barren plains above the waterfalls and the split rocks on the cliffs along the great lake, Culumbi. Next, the memoriam of those taken in the long-suffering war between the three major powers: Crelli, Vigrop, and Bellop. Finally, he ended with the "legend of providence by Jaru" and the discovery of the first dormant eggs of the Visatae.

The eggs marked the newest pivotal point in Crelli history. During the height of the Bellop wars, the discovery of Visatae eggs along the shore of the lake was a newfound curiosity. The discovery of the mysterious eggs, as is the case with most secrets, soon got out, and what was a mystery became a legend. Soon, legend evolved into religion. Crelli would often come to the where the eggs were stored, seeking truth and enlightenment.

An incubation process was developed, and creatures emerged from the shells. The insectoid beings probed the room. Crawling up the back of an unsuspecting Crelli the new species stopped and extended a short appendage toward the skin. The youth gasped as his body shuddered from the puncture to the neck. The pain instantly subsided. The symbiosis was completed successfully and at that moment; the youngling gained volumes of sensory awareness. The Crelli would be changed forever.

The alarmed Crelli was terrified. Leaders from all areas of industry were gathered, probing and testing for any harmful side effects. The youth learned he could detect subtle directions from the attached creature. Through trial and error, a system of separation and reattachment was developed. The ruling class of Jaruvian monks driven by the narcissistic Massari quickly stepped in to "bless" the newfound species as a "gift from Jaru." For the Elders outside the temple, it was providence. The impact changed history for the Crelli. The merger soon led to advancement in all areas.

The radical union upset the balance of the war. No longer were the amphibious Vigrop able to sneak up and catch the Crelli. The number of unwitting Crelli sold in slavery to the Bellop diminished.

The control of the forest now belonged to the Crelli. They finally could take a stand. The cry of "No More" was heard in battle. Younglings were now trained to embrace the symbiotic relationship. At the temples, a new curriculum was created focusing on what one could accomplish if the right Visatae chose them. The intent was to discover the most viable candidates for merging with the Visatae through careful observation and testing by the monks of Jaru in conjunction with the Jamtori.

The Massari quickly organized scores of research teams. Jamtori patrol groups scoured the regions around the lake for more eggs and vespridium.

"Old Raunt is in high spirits this hatching," said Terth's uncle Brawzen. "Get over here and start washing up."

Rhom and Terth made their way over to a shaded area set aside for the prospects, an area of twenty or so small huts placed around the outer edge of the clearing opposite the main entrance of the Rookery. Long-standing trees had grown tall and connected their lattice of branches into a thick blanket of leaves over the stalls. Each hut had a small, shallow stone cistern in the back. A single stool and a stone oven made up the remaining décor. Banners with the family insignia and names of past chosen were strung between two slender posts at the entrance. Each family pod selected their representative for consideration. Some chose the one closest in bloodline from any past Jamtori, others held strict competitions to eliminate the unworthy.

As the two youths approached, they could see Uncle Brawzen. His face was worn and weathered. Despite his age, Brawzen retained his fitness. Massive, sinewed arms protruded from his sleeves like gnarled roots. "Terth my boy, are you sure you want to do this?" Brawzen paused and stoutly squared up in front of Terth.

"The Jamtori are incredible. I want to be part of the strongest force Crellantan has ever known." Terth said. The intense look on his face and confident stance gave little doubt to his determination.

"I've done my best trying to raise you two rascals. Jaru knows you should have had a motherly figure to teach you some manners." Brawzen gave a quick wink to Rhom. "With you gone, it will be only a matter of time before Rhom here is going to pull a crazy stunt to prove he won't be left behind, eh?"

"That's if he gets chosen, Uncle," Rhom replied, looking as solemn as he could. Terth cast a sharp gaze toward Rhom and they both smirked.

"Now, I don't want to let this moment pass before I remind you one more time not all the Jamtori are here for the same reasons. Be cautious about who you trust. I am still not in favor of this choice, Terth, but you are headstrong and determined to see for yourself. Remember, your parents chose to follow the Jamtori and are no longer with us."

"That is exactly why I must do this. I will pass the test and learn the ways of Jamtori. I will be the best and lead the Jamtori Order into a new era of justice." Terth stated with unshakeable clarity.

Brawzen replied, "So be it, and may Jaru guide you to the pinnacle."

Uncle Brawzen always had that peculiar way of cheerfully looking forward, no matter how tough it may seem. Yet, more than once, Rhom had observed the sad look on Brawzen's face whenever they would pass the path to the old labs. Sometimes late at night, he would mumble in his sleep. It was hard for him, losing a sister and her mate. Not to mention taking on two young orphans with wild and adventurous tendencies.

While Terth was inside the hut preparing, Rhom gazed around the clearing. He could see inside the great main doors of the Rookery to the chamber beyond. Visible were the tops of seven opalescent eggs with finely painted gold and red inscriptions. The caretakers inside had cleaned and polished for days, and it showed. The white of the interior blazed in the morning sunlight. The reflections from the decorated eggs were distinct along the bright walls. Rhom knew he would never be chosen to enter that chamber.

As a youngling, he had been smaller than the others. Not to mention his lack of sponsors. His family had been lost in a disaster. When he was young, an explosion decimated a portion of the Proving Grounds containing a research facility nicknamed "The Lab." Terth lost both of his parents and an older sister that day. Rhom had lost his father. His mother had already passed a few months before the explosion. All family pods mourned the considerable number of Crelli who died that day. Brawzen, Terth's uncle, took both younglings under his care, giving them his best. Later Rhom understood from that point on he had lost any chance of being chosen.

Old Raunt bellowed, "The time has come. All Jambat applicants report to the Rookery."

As the candidates made their way to the entrance, an expectant hush crossed the clearing. Rhom studied the group. Some he knew from youth assembly. He could see Sheidel. She had always been a skilled climber. Beyond her was Valden, standing tall and proud, his father boasting to the crowd of their long legacy as elders in the Havens. The ones Rhom did not recognize were trained privately as Terth had been or came from pods that had settled along the fringes of the valley. They were lined up now, fourteen in all. The silence had grown into a pressing roar. Raunt lifted his hands above his head.

For a moment, a slight rustle in the tree above distracted Rhom. "Probably just a snifty looking for nuts," he thought. If he had looked up for a moment longer, he might have seen the quick flick of moving hair and the sparkle of metal on the harness from the figure concealed in the foliage. The shadowed shape settled into a fork in the branches and scanned the clearing as the Masari took position next to old Raunt. The crowd attentively waited for the speech.

"It has been six cycles plus two seasons since our first encounter with the Visatae. Let us not forget our past, for we were once small and timid. Hunted and devoured by the old beasts. Dark were the days of the Crelli, before the emergence, before the great day the ground divided, creating the pool of light at the base of falls. Our progenitors drank the water of light and ate the fruit given to them by the Great Essence, Jaru. Her gift of providence empowered us to defend this valley, to defend her children, the Visatae. Each of you has studied and trained for this moment." Terth's eyes were focused past Old Raunt and on the eggs. Rhom's gaze was a hot line of fire burning through the open gate.

The Masari continued, "On this day we celebrate the union of the chosen and give thanks to the Great Essence for the enlightenment which She provides."

The pressure from the crowd was heavy. The Jambat prospects cleared their minds as Raunt led the group into the egg chamber. The doors were shut.

The door clinked into place with a hint of screeching metal and wood. Terth could see the eggs before him as the group made their way through the annex and into the larger chamber behind. He could feel the weight of the other prospects' eyes as each tried to pierce the veil comprising mental barricades and primal posturing taught to each. He slowly lifted his head ever so slightly to improve his assessment of the group.

Left of Terth, a younger but taller, slight framed, dark-haired prospect named Berendi stood. His family was one of several pods who had moved up the edge of the valley to the west after the division over the accident at the lab. He was wearing a robe adorned with long, vibrant kamburi feathers.

The group filed in and took a position around a large pedestal supporting the eggs. Opposite Terth stood Craznak, a stout, pug-faced Jambat. He had a strong jaw and a low forehead. His limbs were sinewed and thick. He wore a dark, heavy cloth stitched in overlaying patterns of octagonal shapes resembling turtle shells. He had a slight sneer curling up on the left side of his lip. Terth looked down as his eyes connected with the hulking menace before him.

Fourteen selectees charged with anticipation, assessing each other while conducting a silent battle within.

Raunt, carrying a short, nimble rod, approached the group of potentials. "Each of you is granted a choice. That choice will determine your position in the Kindrel."

In the center of the room stood a meter-tall pedestal adorned by seven eggs. Painted on the ground below were two overlapping heptagons, one red and one yellow. Two sets of symbols were repeated in brilliant gold. They represented the foundation of Crelli governance. The seven axioms of the Jamtori: Truthfulness, Morality, Loyalty, Duty, Courage, Honor, and Benevolence. Opposite the main doors, a small dome occupied the space between two dulled milky pillars covered in inscriptions.

The first applicant, a broad-shouldered, dark-haired Jambat named Delpar from the eastern forest control pod, approached the dome and knelt inside. It did not matter who went first. No results would be known until all had been examined. It was only mere moments, and his test was complete. Slowly rising, he walked away to the left and around to the opposite side of the Kindrel.

The inscriptions on the pillars began to faintly glow. The next Jambat approached and knelt. Soon it was Terth's turn. He approached the dome and crawled in. The wavy stone floor was cool. On the ceiling and down the walls, a network of intersecting circles and lines pulsed with a soft blue light. Terth knelt facing the wall opposite the doorway.

He closed his eyes. A gentle warm sensation overcame him, like the feeling one gets when submersing in a bathtub. Terth could feel images forming in his head.

Cloudy, jumbled images faded in and out, never long enough to remember. Brief glimpses of friends, family, and long-forgotten childhood events flashed before his eyes. Suddenly, his mind shifted. An unfamiliar image formed. Terth saw mist swirling about and in the center a shimmering rainbow silhouette, slender and tall. Long thin arms spread wide as if to embrace him. The being called out in a muffled tone that Terth could not understand. He tried to speak but found no voice. The image faded to gray, then darkness and it was done.

Terth stood and walked over to join the rest. "Was it Jaru? Did he see Jaru?" The metal columns glowed. A long thin rod with a small blue round jewel atop emerged from the center of the pedestal which held the eggs. The rod, now extended, glowed with the same blue light as the pillars of the testing area. The blue orb cast a beam on the row of candidates awaiting the results.

Almost in unison, the eggs vibrated as the upper portion of the shells softened and dissolved. The creatures inside pushed out headfirst. The Visatae were symmetrical in form, having hardened nubs along their sides at the center of each segment. Similarly, a beak of hardened skin coming to a point served as an opening or mouth. The larvae Visatae slinked across the floor toward the outer edges of the circle to the Crelli seated along the perimeter, facing away from the eggs. Clicking sounds could be heard as the Visatae drew closer. The long anticipation sent waves of needles across Terth's skin.

The creatures approached the outer ring and contacted the prospects. From the edges of the room, seven monks in gray shimmering robes advanced and knelt behind the Visatae. Reaching out with ornately patterned gloves, the Jaruvian monks lifted the larvae to the level of the individual Crelli's neck above the shoulder line. A small opening along the bottom of the head segment opened. This gap in the creature's anatomy housed the "leash," a spoon-shaped appendage with small needlelike barbs. The leash moved about as if sensing the area. Then, with a flick, it attached itself to the spine of the Crelli.

Placing the Visatae in a pouch on the back of the now-selected Jambat, the monks moved to face the Crelli. Opening a small jar, they inserted their finger into each Crelli's mouth and smeared the substance along the inner gums of the mouth. The concoction affected the young Jambat causing heavy drowsiness. Next, they stretched the chosen Crelli stomach down, allowing the Visatae to fully attach and secure its connection to them.

Seven being a symbolic number to them, the double ratio of candidates to Visatae gave the monks a better pool to choose from. Aptitude scores were determined by the mental capabilities during the test. Those not chosen were ushered out of the room into the annex, where Old Raunt was waiting.

Terth remained face down. The experience of enlightenment combined with victory was thrilling. He had done it. He was now part of the Jamtori. The room was alive with new details. Terth could clearly hear Old Raunt in the annex.

"Life does not end here. Your training to this point has given you an advantage over many Crelli in the Havens. Use your skills to help our kind. Follow the Axioms and heed the voice of Jaru." Raunt said. It was conciliatory no matter how heartfelt and earnest Raunt may be. The choices were made and the unselected prepared to face the greatest rejection, with unknown consequences. They were allotted a time of silence and reflection. Once the monks deemed the group ready, the door would open.

By now, most of the crowd outside the Citadel had eaten an afternoon meal. Vendors packed up the tables and cleaned their areas. Rhom could hear a muffled voice in the back of the crowd. Most likely Blind Teleg impatiently asking for a description of the scene. The afternoon light was low in the trees and Rhom felt himself drifting and melting away.

Then, there it was, the crack of the latch mechanics and the creak of the hinges. The crowd let out their breath in an all-encompassing sigh. Murmurs swirled as one by one the unselected filed out the door and back into the main assembly. The unfortunate headed back to their respective stalls, gathering what strength they could muster to hold their heads high. Rhom peered across the clearing, as each was led down the main stairs, but no Terth. He had done it, somehow; he had been selected. What did the Visatae see in Terth? What quality did he possess that separated him from the other potential candidates? Rhom fervently went through these thoughts while the crowd dispersed.

Soon, the once bustling area surrounding the

training facility was still and somber. Only a few stragglers assigned to sweeping out stalls remained. The silent observer above Rhom slipped away from the clearing, making their way around the edge and up the nearby hillside. Again, Rhom heard the rustle of overhead leaves. He peered into the darkening canopy. The firm grip of Uncle Brawzen's hand on Rhom's shoulder brought him back into the moment.

"Now that Terth is part of the Jamtori, it is time we talked," Brawzen said. "There is something you should know."

Brawzen and Rhom made their way back to the hut they called home. The branches from the tall trees shaded the area and provided extra covering from the elements. The widow, Splincer, shared the clearing. The other dwellings were empty now that the proving grounds had been obliterated. Most had moved downstream from the area and closer to the center of the Havens. Rhom liked the quiet it afforded.

Since Brawzen was not his blood uncle with any expected obligations, this day was an awkward one for the two of them. Rhom was of age and would need to find an occupation. It was possible he could join the Keepers or try his hand at cultivating. When he thought about it, he couldn't see himself doing anything in the Havens. Rhom liked the forest. He liked the smells. He liked the time at the "Cage." No matter what had happened in the past, Terth had always been there with him. Now Terth was gone as part of the Crelli defense force, and Rhom felt out of place.

The late afternoon sun sent hazy beams horizontally across the valley. The air was still and the weight of it pressed upon Rhom as Brawzen spoke.

"My boy, you know I have always watched out for

you and for your part you have made it easy work for a tired Crelli, except for that time you put jindips in the harvest baskets."

"That wasn't me," he replied.

"Maybe not, though I swear to this day, it was you I saw behind the bushes."

Indeed, it had been him that was behind the bushes, although Terth had been the one with the idea. Terth had always had a knack for escaping his uncle's eye.

"Never mind. As I was beginning to say..." Brawzen continued. "You have respected my house and obeyed my wishes these past years and have done well in training, even knowing you would not have a sponsor. Your diligence in our way of life is to be commended. The time has come to pass on what I know about the work your parents were involved with at the Lab in the Proving Grounds."

Rhom tensed at his words. The Lab was not a subject they discussed, ever. It was always in the background. A fog one could feel but not grasp. Rhom had always been too afraid to ask, afraid to relive that awful tragedy again. The two boys had been small, only three cycles. It was hard enough losing his parents. To now talk about it after all this time was unnerving.

"I'm not sure I want to know," Rhom found himself blurting out. He was surprised by his voice.

"I have a responsibility to tell you. Now that Terth is in the Rookery, he will learn soon enough. He is bound to figure it out once he bonds with a Visatae. I had planned on telling you together before today, but I am a selfish old man and did not want to spoil the time I had with you. Now I fear it may be too late."

The afternoon silence now screamed in Rhom's ears. His heart was pounding, and he felt cold.

18

"Rhomazel, you have grown up hearing the stories of the Visatae. The 'gift' of Jaru, the divine connection between Jamtori and Visatae. It's not what it appears to be."

Rhom was unsure what Brawzen was telling him.

"Can the Jamtori do more? Can they read my mind?"

"That is not what I mean." Leaning over the table and peering closer into Rhom's eyes he said, "the Visatae are not from our world, and we are not the first beings to live here." Brawzen leaned back and steadied himself.

"What does that mean? So, what if the Bellop were here first, or the Vigrop, for that matter? What difference does that make? The Visatae were a gift from Jaru, of course. They are from the beyond." Rhom was confused. What did this have to do with his father?

"When my sister Vaetris, Terth's mother, was young, the pods were closer together. The people were still in fear of the Bellop. A new and stronger Sursamain ruled over the eastern Bellop tribes and united them. Drought ravaged the upper plateau beyond the valley ridge. Crelli would disappear from the edges of the forest. The Havens was a way of keeping each other safe. I fought too, like Raunt and Teleg the Blind. We were the Sweepers, Elite Guardians of the Crelli. We would watch from the trees and send warnings when the Bellop approached our part of the forest. The council of elders decided it was best to teach all the younglings as a group in the center of the Havens. The Rookery and Citadel were selected for that purpose."

"But I thought the Rookery was built for the eggs and was tended by the acolytes of Jaru?" Rhom replied.

"It has always been a refuge for the followers of Jaru. The Acolytes of Jaru were our instructors before the

Bellop Wars, before the Jamtori." Brawzen said.

"Ok?" Rhom was still confused.

"I will tell you how it changed. When they were pups, about one cycle and six seasons, your father, Terth's father, and a few others would often play tricks on us. Moving branches or making strange noises to try and fool us into sounding the alert. Your father's favorite was sneaking up a tree silently as possible so as not to be seen. He would then try to steal lunch from one of us. We loved it. The actions of these younglings kept us alert and sharp. I think for those boys, it made them more confident and daring." Brawzen paused for a moment. A wave of happiness crossed his face. Rhom too felt uplifted as he pictured some of the tricks that Terth and he had tried to play on Uncle Brawzen growing up.

"Now, where was I?" Brawzen's face dimmed, and his refocused gaze was direct. "One day, their group gave us the slip and traveled north along the water's edge up to the big lake Culumbi. Heavy rain had fallen for several days. The water was high, and it was windy. Waves of unusual size formed upon the lake. As a result, portions of the cliffs on the far side of the lake broke off into the water. Debris along the shoreline made an exciting place for adventurous younglings to explore." He stopped for a moment to swish his cup, took his left hand, brushed out his whiskers along his jaw, and resumed.

"What they found that day changed the Crelli's future. Eggs like the ones in the Rookery." He paused and looked deeply at Rhom. "Eggs and something else...a new kind of gummy, floating rock. At first, there were only a few clumps. Each boy took some home and hid it away somewhere near his hut or pod. One in the group, I think it was a boy named Brimble, no Bendohl, maybe Berhpas—the name escapes me. Anyway, he decided to sleep near his new prize. A few days later he started having strange dreams. In his dreams, he would see himself in his room sleeping. He also noticed that he could hear other things beyond that room as well. Not clear though, it was muffled, like being trapped under a large blanket."

Rhom was starting to feel cold. "What does this have to do with my parents?"

"I'm getting to that, be patient."

Rhom sighed and leaned back a little. The warm afternoon was now getting to him, and he began to feel prickly.

"Soon the unexpected happened. The rock was softening up. The boys had an idea of bringing all the material together into one place and exposing it to greater heat. Within a brief time, all the rocks melted together into one mass. The glob of former rocks was now hot to the touch and had become sticky. They made their way back to the shoreline of Lake Culumbi to gather all the gummy rock they could carry.

"Well, boys being boys, the secret did not last long. A council was formed, the discovery was brought before them, and a decision was made. For the good of the community, the Crelli must not know about this until more could be learned. The High Elders called on the Monks of Jaru for their input.

"Jaru has given us this element for some purpose. For what purpose is yet unknown, but in our divine connection to Jaru, insight will be provided.' The monks' position would not be swayed."

"So, then Jaru did provide this new element," Rhom replied.

"That element was Vespridium..."

"The source of all of our energy," Rhom thought.

"...and what it truly is, is something far more

dangerous than the Jamtori and the Monks of Jaru want you to know." Uncle Brawzen seemed to be choosing his words.

"Your father knew the truth. He and the others were offered a deal. They were to be the next group of Jambat at the selection that season in exchange for their silence. One peep and all involved would disappear." Uncle Brawzen stood up and checked the door and the rear hatch at the side of the firepit. Convinced, he sat down and continued.

"After the rigged selection of the new Jambat was completed, the group was given a special secret assignment. I know this because as an Elite Guard, I had access to all areas of the Citadel and Rookery. The area occupied by this group became known as the Proving Grounds. A lot of resources were used to build up defenses, walls were built, and tunnels were hewn deep into the rock face of the river cliffs. Vigrop were seen slinking through the southern gate with packs over their slimy scaled backs. We were told the Monks had seen a vision, a new age for the Crelli, an age of dominion and peace over the valley. The Vigrop sightings were merely "emissaries" meeting the council at the new stronger facility inside the Proving Grounds. The Crellans found hope and joy in this. It was a false hope. A group opposed to the use of the Visatae tried to bring an end to the research, calling it an atrocity and a perversion to Jaru."

Sweat had begun to form on Rhom's palms and along the back of his neck. "But the history we learned at training, the victory over the valley, and the defeat of the Bellop. Why would you send Terth there?"

"Our history…" Brawzen replied. "Our history is fractured, and it began when the first Visatae egg cracked open. I had no choice with Terth. The Jamtori wanted him.

I can't go against them, but I can save you. Do you know what happens to a Jamtori when they lose connection to the Visatae? Insanity. Teleg put out his own eyes when he lost his. I don't want you to see Terth that way. It almost happened to me."

"But you...you're ok...right? Rhom was gripping the edge of the table.

"I had something to help. Your father and the others gave me something. It was an ingestible form of Vespridium, that very same rock they had found. It calmed me and allowed me to break the addiction. The monks now give the Jambat smaller doses at the beginning of their merger." Rhom relaxed and breathed again. Brawzen went on. "The truth is that serum is both good and evil. Too much and you can be sick. That's what happened to your mother. Too little and the madness is not abated. It is said an overdosed Jamtori caused the explosion at the proving grounds."

"My mother? My mother? She wasn't a drug-addicted lab experiment."

"Not technically, but she was one of the first to try the serum. Your father tried his best to stop her, but she insisted on sampling each variation only in slight doses. However, over time, it was too much.

"It's not possible!" Rhom couldn't believe it. How could his mother be involved in something so profane?

"Rhom, you have to understand we only saw the benefits that came from their research." Brawzen was trying desperately to get him to understand. "The wheel works at the river, the podlamps in the villages, the fruit houses. Even the modern Monsu units. None of this would be possible without the efforts of your parents and others like them. Terth will be fine with the Jamtori. He is determined."

Rhom was so confused. "What about the lies to the people? What about working with those detestable Vigrop?"

"Many gladly risked their lives with the hope of a better place for their families. You must understand. The Crelli may be peaceful now, but during the Bellop Wars, it was not the same." Brawzen sighed "Rhom, isn't it enough to know that your parents gave their lives to ensure peace for all Crelli?"

"No! It isn't, and it never will be!" Rhom jumped up from the table and left the room, grabbing his jerkin.

"Wait Rhom, there is more you must know before it is too late. The Visatae are up to something. I need your help. Terth isn't alone..."

Rhom left the hut and leaped from the platform. The world around him became a swirling mass of gray and burgundy as he rolled through the air. His arm shot out, grabbing a branch, the momentum vaulting him deep into the trees. As he moved through the dense canopy, his thoughts clashed. He had always been taught the Visatae/Crelli merger was spiritual. Yet now the elder who raised him, his only connection to the pod, was telling him it was not so. It was too much. He moved faster, trying to outrace his thoughts. It was no use. Finally, alighting to a slender branch, out of breath, and still confused, he stopped.

The few remaining rays of light could be seen on the peaks at the eastern side of the valley near the Bellop border. Rhom felt the slight change in temperature as the breeze rolled down the hillside. Long shadows danced as smaller branches swayed in the wind. His stomach growled. Arching up from the branch and shaking his arms out, he looked around to realize this was an unfamiliar part of the forest. Hoping to get a better view, he began the ascent to clear the canopy, only to feel a tug. Something was wrapped around his foot. He hadn't noticed it at first. Looking down, he saw the shiny scales of a cornas. Rhom and Terth had often seen the discarded skins of cornas hanging in the branches and had teased the smaller ones near the Cage. They had even tried to keep one as a pet, but the enclosure they had made was broken and empty when they returned to feed it.

This cornas was much larger than any they had encountered before. The girth of the tentacle around his leg was thicker than both his hands could wrap around. That tentacle wasn't the only trouble, it was the spiked tongue one had to watch out for.

Small barbs lined the edge, each full of paralyzing venom. One sting and he would be numb and limp in moments. The beast's two other limbs were wrapped around a lower branch; its mouth was open wide, tongued whip ready to strike.

The distance between him and the cornas was closing as the creature pulled Rhom's leg closer. He locked his arms around the branch he was on, holding with all his might. The weight of the large tentacle combined with the power behind it was proving too much for Rhom to handle. Oh, how he wished his feelings had not gotten the best of him. Why had he fled so far into the forest? He blamed Terth for being chosen and leaving him behind. This never would have happened if Terth were here. During the mere seconds that had expired, the distance was lessening as the monster below loosened his anchorage to reach its prey and strike that deadly blow.

Hope was fading. Rhom had to do something, anything, to preserve his life. The cornas began a series of strategic yanks to loosen Rhom's grip. The branch Rhom was holding began to creak and pop. It was all going to be over soon. Suddenly, he had an idea. Timing the tugs made by the beast, Rhom began pulling on the branch. It was a dangerous gamble, but it might work. The creaks grew louder as the branch's sway increased. Then with a crack, the branch broke and tumbled.

Taking advantage of the slack, he wrapped his legs and arms, riding past the creature still attached to his leg. The cornas lashed out with his deadly poison apparatus, striking Rhom in the upper thigh. The jagged edge of the branch gouged the monster across the anchored limb. Gray ooze immediately flowed from the gash, and the beast released his grip for a moment.

It was enough. Rhom relaxed his hold and haphazardly leaped as far as he could. He crashed through the branches and rolled down the hillside as the falling branch continued to tumble down away from Rhom, the crushed cornas in tow. The carpet of leaves, twigs, and wet debris did not slow him down. Now sliding on his back, headfirst, and gazing at the trees above him, Rhom could sense the poison taking effect. Powerless, he continued down the slope, gaining speed as the angle increased. His heart paused as he was launched through the air. The silence was followed by a splash, then darkness.

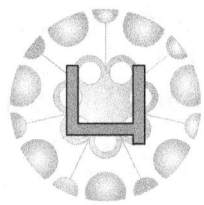

"Yereni! Yeeereniiiiii!!! Where has that girl gone to now?" called Mallahen. "Bendohl, have you seen Yereni?"

"Shh, not now. I am trying to focus." Bendohl was hunched over a small round table. Upon the table, small tools were spread out. At the center, a small device resembling an acorn glowed faintly.

"If she doesn't show up soon, her dinner will be cold, not to mention she hasn't collected any samples this week. Honestly, I don't know what to do with that girl."

"Patience, my dear, you have to let our flower grow in her own time."

"Well, I wish it was sooner rather than later," sighed Mallahen.

Then the door burst open. "Poppa, today was the hatching!"

At the sound of the interruption, Bendohl dropped the acorn-shaped device, causing it to shatter into pieces. "Confound it!" Looking up with a scowl, he stared at the two of them. "Now I have to start over."

Briefly glancing toward him and forgetting all about

dinner and the fact Yereni was late, Mallahen turned back to her daughter and said, "Did you see it? How about the candidates? Were any of them handsome?"

As Yereni opened her mouth to reply, her father cut in. "What were you doing down there? Did anybody see you? Were you followed? How many times have we discussed this? The Citadel is dangerous. Their ways are not ours. They have lost their way."

"It's okay Poppa, I was careful. I hid in the trees above their heads. Nobody saw me, I promise." Yereni twirled around the table to a basket of fruit and grabbed one from the top. Tossing it into the air, she caught it with her mouth as she flitted out the door to the rooms behind.

"Now wait a minute, young lady, we are not through." Bendohl said. Mallahen put her arm out and stepped in front of him.

"Our flower is growing in her own time," Mallahen said, trying her best to mimic his voice.

"Bah! As long as she doesn't become a weed..." He snuffed, turning to collect his work from the ground.

Turning back to the now cold meal left on the table, Mallahen could not hide the slight sideways smile as she thought back to her days in the village, seeing all the brave Jamtori returning from the wars, and hoping to catch an eye. She remembered Bendohl, how young and bold he was, so full of ideas and dreams. He would spend hours discussing the Proving Grounds and the discoveries they had made. Now he spent his time brooding over the fire. Failure at Lab and the tragedy from the explosion had driven him from the pods and society. She had thought the retreat to the forest would be temporary. His pursuit of the old ways and the rekindled faith in Jaru, the Provider, had improved his demeanor for a time, but the pain of loss twisted his devoted faith into a prison of absolutes.

Duty said she could not leave. She had a daughter to raise .Yereni was the light she needed to feel alive. Even if that light would sometimes burn the edges of her heart along its journey.

Stepping out the rear of the communal area and through the small antechamber full of drying herbs and shelves stocked with sealed jars of fruit, nuts, and edible leaves, Mallahen exited their home and entered the clearing behind. The twinkle of the night's first stars could be seen on the still surface of the water in the stone basin at the center. The blanket over her heart lifted as she cast her eyes across the night sky.

There was a night like this long ago when she had been the one twirling around the room carefree. It was a night when the thoughts of adventure, boys, and fun far overshadowed the cautious words of her father. Oh, what would her life be now if she had only heeded his advice? Mallahen would be married to the lead cook at the Citadel markets, fat and worry-free. A chuckle came to the surface. No, she had made her choice and had no regrets. Yereni was special and needed guidance, and Mallahen was determined to see it through. "Tomorrow is a new day," she breathed. "Start again and be firm. Yereni needs your guidance," she told herself. Straightening her stance, she turned and headed up to bed.

"Wake up, sleepyhead." Mallahen gently brushed her daughter's cheek. Yereni stirred. The new morning air from the window was crispy. "You need to get an early start today and complete your chores from yesterday. Later we can sit in the garden, and you can tell me all about the gathering. I'll make you your favorite. Just don't tell your father. He will say I'm indulging you."

Yereni sat up, stretched her arms, blinked, pulled the blanket over her head, and curled back into the bed. There was no way she was going to do chores when her bed was so warm and toasty. Her mother pulled the blanket back and clasped her hands around Yereni's. Sitting Yereni up, Mallahen stared at her daughter. "This is no time to sleep after sneaking down to the valley like you did yesterday. Now get up and get started before I change my mind and make you borschenda," which happened to be Yereni's least favorite meal.

"Ok, ok." Tossing on her favorite pink and maroon jerkin with a gray harness over it, she made her way over to the tool hut. Grabbing a pair of tonsu and monsu, she strapped them on.

At the beginning of the Visatae era, towards the middle of the Bellop Wars, tonsu and the accompanying monsu were developed as a simple form of defense and mode of travel through the dense jungle surrounding the Crelli lands. The tonsu were spikes that were strapped to the outer calf. Hand controls were used extend and retract the tonsu spike. The pneumatic force of the spike had multiple benefits. It gave the Crelli the ability to leap higher when activated. One could rapidly climb large trunks by using the spike. In combat, it was combined with kicks to break through the tough hides and shields of the Bellop. The monsu served the same purpose but were attached along the outer forearm. The controls were managed by a series of rings attached to the fingers. Mounted to a Crelli harness was a small device that regulated the power of the system.

The new Jambat trainees down in the Rookery would learn using the upgraded vespridium-powered model with lethal precision. There was a time when all

Crelli would have been equipped, but the efficiency of the Jamtori force gave everyone a sense of peace. Bendohl had insisted his daughter learn the old ways and depend upon her own strength.

Yereni exited the hut and bounded across the clearing, then leaped high into the trees. Racing across the branches. Yereni loved the open air. A smile crossed her face as she gracefully traveled. Her "chores" were simple enough. Search the edges of Lake Culumbi and collect samples of the soil, leaves, and spore of the small creatures. She was not supposed to follow the lake south, but stay west and north, and never past the forest edge near the wastelands. In addition, "Never drink from the lake because you might be seen." Her father had said. In the beginning, she had obeyed, but more recently she began roaming, edging increasingly south. These days she almost headed straight toward the pod settlements near the south shore and the clearings of the Havens along the streams that flowed from the outlet of the lake and along the valley floor.

Surely there was no harm in watching. After all, they were Crelli like her. What was the big deal? Just because Father wanted to live away from the pods, why should she have to? Still, a fear of the unknown kept her from getting too close. Yereni would make every effort to conceal among the foliage. Today she planned on returning to the area near the large dome where she had seen the young Crelli being selected.

Across the western ridge and down the northern slope towards the lake, her rapid pace amongst the trees could be heard as a whoosh accompanied by a whistle of metal upon metal from the tonsu projecting in and out. The movements were efficient, and she left little evidence behind along her path. Yereni noticed a few radoacs circling the stream crossing ahead. She slowed her pace and turned off the compressor on her back. She pressed herself against the trunk of the tree she was on and listened. Not noticing any noises of unusual origin, she then slid down to the forest floor. Ahead of her and down the slope at a dark shallow pool partially hidden by a carved-out dome of rock, the radoacs had gathered. A flurry of wings, tails, and heads flipping, darting, dodging, and hopping caused a sort of enchanting dizziness as her eyes struggled to peer past the tempest of beasts and view the source of the commotion.

Realizing what lay before her, Yereni let out a shrill chirping noise as she lunged forward while flipping on the compressor again as she crossed the distance of the clearing. Yereni leaped across the final ten yards and landed right in the middle of the mass of creatures.

Not much bigger than an iguana, the radoacs disliked fighting their prey, choosing rather to eat the weak or near dead; they scattered only to rest amongst the branches and screech down at her. A few dove in and swirled around her, artfully staying out of reach. Yereni made a quick thrust upward. The monsu on her right forearm sprang out, piercing a radoac through the belly. She quickly brought her arm down as the spike retracted. The action shook the now-dying beast from the blade, sending it tumbling across the leafy carpet. She looked about as the radoacs backed away from the clearing, hissing, and bobbing their heads in a back-and-forth swaying motion. Some made their way up the trees and out into the sky above in search of a new meal.

Pulling back her hood, she reached out and felt the forehead of the wounded Crelli. It was warm. Next, she leaned down, placing her cheek next to the mouth to feel for breath. A slight tingle and a gentle movement of wind along her cheek let her know they were still alive. Skirting the edge of the pool, she dragged the body near to the rock overhang, keeping an eye on the clearing. With the solid stone to her back, Yereni could now take a better look at what, or more precisely, who, she was looking at. It was a Crelli for sure, more than that she did not know. The radoacs had only started their work. Bite marks, small tears, and slices covered the poor victim's arm, legs, and head. The body had been lying face down in a tuft of reeds along the pool edge and therefore not readily accessible at first. A dark hole could be seen above the ankle and the surrounding skin was turning green.

He was alive, but barely. The scales tipped favorably to the hands of death rather than the arms of life. It would be difficult to move him, but Yereni could do nothing more where they were. She needed a safe place and access to her mother's containers and vials. It was clear from the smelly ooze and discolored mark on his leg that it was poison. She fashioned a sled from a fallen tree nearby. Tearing away a large piece of bark, she formed a crude skiff strapping the fallen Crelli's harness as a lead. Rolling him onto the bark, she stood up and began the tolling task of toiling up the hill.

The Jaruvian Monks were disciplined. Terth was not used to the silence they so loudly projected in the Citadel grounds. The inner awakening experienced by his interaction with the Visatae gave everything greater depth and volume. All motion was slowed. Every action could be seen like many compiled photos arrayed in succession. He had only to pick one and every detail would be brought forward in vivid display. Sound, color, and smell became corporeal, as thick as gelatin. Waves of sensations flooded Terth's mind. The monks had devised a mixture of herbs and extracts to dull the experience to the level of tolerance specific to the individual.

As the sustained imbuement of elements in the mixture took their effect, Terth found it easier to select the sense he wanted to extend. He found he could hear conversations outside the compound when the main stalls were occupied. Patterns on leaves, textures on the walls, and petals of flowers all became intricate and ornate designs even from afar. The one downfall was taste. The richer the food, the worse it was. The consensual theory was since the Visatae were unable to translate taste, this caused a type of mental feedback. The Jambat ate a plain diet of mashed yarba root along with the "Spirit of Jaru," which helped them control the experience.

The Jambat units slept in circular rooms below ground, northeast of the main gate and across the center yard from the selection chamber. The chamber was arrayed in such a way that the head of each bed was in the center, like the spokes of a wheel. A column occupied the middle of the room. This column contained an overhanging circular platform about 3 meters from the floor. At night, the Visatae would ascend to the upper platform and congregate, squirming and clicking as they swarmed over meals provided by the monks. The separation provided a rest period for the tired trainees. On the floors above them, the seasoned Jamtori slept similarly, in groups of seven all heads in the center. However, it was their duty to hunt and prepare the food of their own Visatae.

It was morning and time to assemble. Each Jambat had a particular location to stand for pretraining meditation. The formation was a larger version of the testing Kindrel without a center pedestal. Based on the symbols of the Axiom, the Jambat aligned with the points in a circular formation facing inward. Lines embedded in the courtyard stone formed the connections between each point. According to the point assigned that day, they were required to recite the corresponding truths from the Axiom. Today, Terth was assigned to Benevolence. Old Raunt strolled across the compound, making his way toward the awaiting Jambat.

"You are the 28th Order of Jambat since the Awakening and the 52nd patrol group since the beginning of the Bellop Wars. Many before you have been where you stand now. Some did not take this training seriously and paid with their lives. I expect you to remember this during your drills today and focus." Raunt was exceptionally grumpy in the morning. The rumor was the scar on his chest was deeper than it looked, and the inner part of the skin had hardened and would rub across his ribs when the air was cold, resulting in his terrible mood. He continued, "There is no shortcut to arduous work, not a trick I haven't seen, or a place in this Citadel where you can hide. I know everything and you better not forget it."

The Masari of the Jaruvian Order came in after Raunt. His calm demeanor diffused some of the tension. In his hand, he carried a short nimble rod ready to inflict quick justice on the shoulders of young Jambat, who fell out of line. His judgments were swift, but fair.

"My children," the Masari began, "clear your mind, relax your body, let the guidance of the Visatae connect you with your surroundings and through them understand the providence of Jaru."

The Jambat knelt on their assigned locations, facing inward to the center of the circle where the Masari stood, eyes closed. Raunt walked along the outer edge behind them in a clockwise pattern.

The first Axiom was Truthfulness. Today it was Delpar, which was awkward for Terth because he had not learned to trust him yet. Delpar began, "I am the eye of Jaru. I must be open in my judgments. Jaru knows my inner thoughts, therefore I cannot hide from Jaru. The Visatae sense my thoughts. My words must be true."

Next was Craznak, who was assigned Morality. "I am the hand of Jaru. I must be steady in my decisions. Jaru knows my inner feelings. Therefore, I cannot hide from Jaru. The Visatae know my intentions. My intentions must be righteous," he recited.

Following Craznak was Sheidel. She was known for

36

her swift climbing abilities. Her favorite pastime before coming to the hatching had been chasing jindips across the treetops until finally catching one and petting its belly until it fell asleep an act only a few could do on the luckiest day. Today she was selected for Loyalty. Sheidel recited, "I am the heart of Jaru. Jaru has chosen the Visatae to guide me, therefore I choose to protect the Visatae. The Jamtori and Visatae are one. We are one with Jaru."

After her was Moori. Raised at the lakeside pods, he was a mystery. Silent and still, others often forgot he was even there. He started his Axiom for duty. "I am the feet of Jaru. I must not forsake my responsibility. Jaru has not forsaken us. I will not forsake the Crelli. The Visatae are steadfast. I will be dedicated to my work." He completed the pledge.

Only two more to go and it would be Terth's turn. He relaxed his body and cleared his thoughts as the sensations brought to him by his connection to the Visatae pulsed through him. He could hear the words of the next Axiom.

"I am the strength of Jaru. I must be fearless. Jaru is an eminent provider. The Visatae is the gift of Jaru. A gift of power. I have no fear while I am Jamtori," the Jambat assigned to Courage recited.

"Courage, yeah I'm gonna need strength to get through this day if I mess up," Terth was thinking. One more to go and it would be his turn.

Berendi was next to Terth and began his Axiom for Honor. "I am the pride of Jaru. I was chosen by Jaru to be her warrior. The Visatae selected me. I have been honored. I will not betray the honor of Jaru."

Finally, it was Terth's turn. "Benevolence, I am the mouth of Jaru. I must be compassionate to the Crelli. Jaru is the provider, therefore I will care for the Crelli.

37

The Visatae have blessed me with the awakening. I will give to those less fortunate in the name of Jaru." There it was done. Everyone did their part with no mistakes. It was the first day and no mistakes. Raunt, still grumpy, stopped his pacing, looked at them, then only grunted as he walked across the yard to the fountain for a drink. Masari opened his eyes and scanned the circle.

"Interesting, but we shall see," he said as he relaxed his grip, letting the tip of his rod slide across the stone yard. "Yes, we shall see."

Wiping the last few drops of water from his chin, Raunt made his way to the center of the Kindrel. "Well, well, muckworms, are you ready to begin the real test?" His good eye gleamed brightly in the morning sun. He continued, "Now that you have had a taste of the bigger world, it is time you paid the fee. Now scurry up the tower and feed your pet. If something happens to them, it will be worse for you."

The Jambat silently left the yard, lined up, and ascended the stairs to their berths and ready room. A new jumpsuit and harness lay at the end of each of their beds. The cloth was a gray and light tan mixture of slight variations in a pattern of perfect day or night camouflage. The harness went over the shoulders, coming down to a "Y" with a loop to pass a belt through. A thermos-like canister and power unit was attached to the back. The canister was designed to comfortably house the Visatae as well as protect it from harm. Once donning the harness, the Jambat would then connect the Monsu and Tonsu. Finally, a short cloak with a hood covered it all. Worn pulled back over the right shoulder, a dark dull metal clasp in the shape of the Heptagonal Kindrel held the cloak together.

The group prepared silently. Reaching up to the

platform above their beds, they gently rubbed the back of their Visatae to stimulate movement and alert them for the reconnection. It was now time to place them in the chambers on the back of the harness. Closing the lid with a twist, the Visatae extended a flexible bristle-sided needle out a small hole and made direct contact with the skin along the spine. Terth could feel the bristles along his neck and then bam! The kaleidoscope of colors, smells, and sounds hit him.

As the others connected, he started to pick up on their activity. It was not thoughts he sensed, but rather the intention of the group. He could feel what another Jambat was about to do moments before they did it. With training, the team would learn to function as one, knowing the orientation of each member and acting to benefit the whole, especially in combat.

Terth heard a ball bouncing off the wall at tremendous speed. He sensed simultaneously who had thrown the ball and what direction it was rebounding. He ducked as the ball passed over his head from behind. Reaching into a bag he pulled out another one. Five more balls bounced off the wall as Terth threw his.

Soon the room was filled with bouncing balls ricocheting off walls and colliding mid-air. The team ducked and dodged, snatching balls from the air and redirecting them.

"Drop a ball or get tagged and you're out." Terth said. The game continued for some time until finally Terth won. The last ball tagged Delpar just below the elbow. Standing up Terth grinned. "Today I get to lead the team on the patrol." Terth said.

"Agreed, but I'm going to win tomorrow." Delpar replied.

"You can try." Terth said.

"You are not alone." A soft, shimmery voice whispered.

The sound was like the breeze in the trees. Rhom could feel the voice around him and through him. He could see the outline of the forest canopy and the sky beyond. The voice seemed beyond the sky and yet somehow near, almost inside him.

"You are not alone," he heard again.

"Who are you?" Rhom questioned.

"I am the mother of the heavens," the shimmer replied. "I am the source of life. I will bring you peace."

"The Provider," Rhom asked. "Are you Jaru?"

"You may call me so if it pleases you. I am the Mother."

Rhom could barely make out a silhouette leaning over him. A wide range of colors slowly swirled, pulsing irregularly through a wide gambit of brightness temperature. He tried to sit up, only to find he could not move his body. He told himself to move, but his body was not listening. Waves of energy pressed him to the ground.

"I have seen your spark and heard your call across

the void. Your pain is terrible. I can relieve you. You are not alone" The voice was less ethereal now, yet as near and far as before.

Frustrated with not being able to move, Rhom turned his energy toward his other faculties. His hearing seemed ok. He could hear water lapping along a shoreline; it seemed nearby. His eyes were open as he had already seen the canopy and the stars. What about smell? Rhom attempted to inhale a deep breath through his nostrils. Nothing. He wasn't breathing.

"Where am I?" he cried out. "Why can't I move? Who are you? Show yourself!"

"I am the Mother; I can remove the pain. You are not alone. " The shadowy figure flickered. Color and form replaced the darkened outline. The voice transitioned again. A familiar face became clear.

"Mother?" Rhom was confused. How was this possible?

"I am the Mother, I am... Your... Mother."

The shifting colors slowly aligned to form the outline of a face. He could see her now. Nothing had changed. She looked exactly the way he remembered.

"Momma, where are we?" he asked

"You called to me, and I came. You are not alone," she replied calmly.

As Rhom was about to ask again where he was, a bright flash broke the moment, followed by darkness and pain. The sky dimmed, and the figure faded.

"Momma!" he cried out.

"You are not alone," he heard. But his mother was gone. The shimmery echo could still be heard. Once again, a flash and pain.

"Lay still while I set your foot, you wild jindip" Yereni snapped.

41

Rhom opened his eyes. The sky was bright. He blinked several times to adjust to the light. His head was pounding, and his body was sore all over. He felt his heart beating. The smell of forest vegetation filled his nose.

"Alive" Rhom thought to himself. Again, a flash crossed his eyes and a shooting pain raced up his leg.

"Oww" he cried.

"Almost done, you ninny. Sit still!" she replied.

"That hurts!" he responded.

"You are lucky I found you when I did. Lying face down in a pool covered in filth and cornas goo. The radoacs would have already been done with and you would be nothing but bones by now if it wasn't for me. It would seem you owe me a thank you." Yereni crossed her arms and looked as tough as she could.

The word cornas brought it all back to him, the struggle in the trees, sliding down the hill, the water. He tried to sit up. His leg was still numb. He looked down. What a mess. Arms matted with blood, dirt, and debris; the girl had covered the larger ones with a purple poultice. Rhom noticed his harness had been cut and used to set the ankle, so violently wrenched in the tree battle. He was a wreck.

"Thank you," he sheepishly said.

"Where is your pod? What part of the Havens are you from?" Yereni knew she was breaking all her father's rules by talking with him. She had done the right thing rescuing him, but now she was heading full speed into direct opposition to all the foundational rules laid out by her parents. What was she supposed to do, patch him up and leave? He could still die. Also, she had seen his face yesterday at the Hatching. He had stood right below her. She even suspected once that he had seen her. Now he was here in the forest near her home. The curiosity was too great.

"Well, if you must know. I am from the West Haven pods outside the Rookery. My name is Rhomazel. What about you?"

"Err, I am from nearby. I live with my parents beyond the boundary. My name... "she paused. "My name is not important right now. What is important is how we are going to move you to a safer place." Yereni had dodged a bullet there. "Never let others know more about you than you do about them," her father would say. "You can't trust anyone."

Rhom looked around. He could see the drag marks along the forest floor, away from the pool and under the safety of the rock shelf. They were now above the pool, tucked into a fork of roots to a large tree. Rhom was lying on a piece of long bark. A portion of the shredded harness was still tied to one end.

"Can you move your other leg? If you can stand, we can move together up the hill. Do you see the old Jamtori scout tower over there. That's where I found the salve for your cuts."

"Give me your tonsu and strap them on either side of my leg above the knee." He said.

"No way," Yereni said and jumped back.

"C'mon, I can't exactly run away and unless you want to carry me on your back all the way uphill, I can't think of a better idea. Can you?"

"Well, I don't want the ick smell from your filthy clothes rubbing off on me. anyway." She wrinkled her nose, squinted her eyes, turned, and stuck her tongue out.

Rhom was a pathetic sight and truthfully, he did smell something fierce. Feeling a little foolish for getting lost in the forest but awkwardly grateful for being rescued by a girl, he quickly responded, "Well then let's get on with it. Hand me your gear."

Unlatching her harness and tonsu, Yereni handed over the gear, leaving her monsu still strapped to her forearms. Rhom wrapped the devices securely around his leg and adjusted the harness straps to fit his frame. He flipped the dial and locked the extended tonsu rods. He could now use the spikes to keep his wounded leg above the ground. His muscles were lethargic, but they were able to work their way up the hill to the abandoned shelter.

Rhom leaned against the base of the tree as Yereni made her way up the tree to the shelter platform. A few moments later, a looped rope dangled above Rhom's lap. He placed his good foot into the stirrup and grabbed onto the rope. The creaking sound of winch and tackle could be heard as he slowly ascended. Climbing through the hatch and rolling over onto his back, Rhom was exhausted.

Yereni left out a "hmpf" and said, "It's not over yet stinkball. You need to get clean and disinfected before you can rest."

The roof of the shelter was equipped with a rainwater collector. A gravity-powered cistern and filtration system provided the occupant's clean water. Yereni filled a container and brought it over to Rhom. She poured it over his hands as he started removing the layers of dirt, blood, muck, and just plain filth. The darkened water spilled upon the decking around the outpost and down through the cracks, swirling and dissipating as it made its way to the forest floor. This building was designed to house four Jamtori during a time of heightened war. Upper and lower bunks could be found to the left of the entrance, and a table and cooking pylon to the right. The far wall contained lockers for provisions and emergency supplies. A small platform above the beds was added later to provide a place for the Visatae.

With the Vigrop Pact in place, the southern forest was not considered a strategic point, and the focus had been turned to reinforcing the valley floor between the Havens and Lake Culumbi. Rhom and Yereni made effective use of the now-unoccupied space. Now clean and somewhat feeling better, Rhom could climb into a lower bunk and sleep.

It was at this moment Yereni remembered her chores. Popping up, she grabbed her harness and belongings and ran for the hatch.

"I have to go, but I'll be back to check on you soon."

Rhom replied, "I will be fine. I just need to sleep."

Yereni was curious still about this Crelli, and why he was in her part of the forest. "I will be back. Stay put. It is still unsafe for you to travel."

Opening the cover, she dove toward the supporting tree and stabbed into the trunk with her monsu. Springing off into a backflip, she cleared the shadow of the outpost and landed lightly on an opposing tree. She looked to her left as she again sprung away, this time heading north and downhill toward the river.

Rhom was now alone. His thoughts turned to the vision he had. A vision he was undecided upon. Was it truly his mother? If it was indeed her, where was she? The being had said that they were Jaru, but when the shape solidified in front of him, it did look like his mother. It was exactly how she had looked the last time Rhom had seen her happy and healthy. Not how she had been during those last painful days, but more how she looked on his third solstice. There was more. Rhom also had to confront the words spoken by Uncle Brawzen. The Visatae were evil? Then why let Terth even train to be a Jambat? Why not leave and hide in the hills with the other Jaru purists? Again, there were too many unanswered questions. His head hurt and he was tired. Part of him wanted to sleep, the other part was afraid to do so. Sleeping might mean another visit from his mother, or it might mean something even more terrible. His body, however, found victory over his mind and Rhom was finally asleep.

A pair of tired hands gently folded a small worn tunic and returned it to an open chest. Setting a harness and a Kamburi feather on top, Uncle Brawzen closed the lid. Sitting back with a sigh, he scanned the room, remembering two small boys he brought home years ago. They were sad, worn out, and scared. Who wouldn't be?

That first night had been a long one. He closed his eyes to better recall the image of those two younglings. The glazed looks in their eyes, broken expressions projecting the shards of the shattered souls inside. Brawzen had to decide that night. "Do I keep them here and raise them? Would it be better to pass them off to the monks? Surely, they would be better suited to care for these two."

Brawzen had been drained; his spirit was empty. Alone, he was alone. No parents, no mate, no siblings, just these two babes. He should give them away to the monks and disappear. Everything in his broken heart said run, run, and don't look back. What would an ex-soldier know about raising younglings, anyway? He was not a mother, nor had he ever been a parent. The dilemma weighed heavily on the already frail state he was in.

He peered down at the small face of his nephew, Terth. The pattern of lines along the cheeks, the lips, and even his eyebrows looked exactly like Brawzen's sister Vaetris. She had been half his age, but twice as bold. Her brave curiosity led her straight into the arms of an equally inquisitive Crelli who would become Terth's father. Why did she have to be a part of those stupid tests? She was a mother and a spouse.

It was all because of the council—the council, and those experiments. Brawzen had served in the Bellop Wars during its height. The now completely functional Jamtori equipped with a Visatae guide had gained victory after victory in the forest, driving the ferocious Bellop east away from the river and up the valley toward the far mountain ridge. He knew full well what the council was like. These two pups should be far from the influence of the Elders.

Maybe taking them to the monks wasn't such a good idea. He had heard rumors of a new social movement growing in the northern glens. A group of Crelli purists had rejected the Visatae as an abomination and not the "Gift of Jaru," as the monks proclaimed. Leaving their pods behind, the group was preparing to migrate deep into the forest to live off the land without tools or shelter. They were embracing the land, free from inhibitions. Perhaps he should have taken the two young orphans to find this group of bohemians.

Long into the night, he considered the past. The cool dew had settled, and the air was still. It was the last gasp of night before the light changed and the galloping rays of morning light would pan the forest.

Returning to the present, Brawzen opened his eyes, stood up, and walked to the front room. Grabbing a pack of supplies, he exited the dwelling, looking up toward the sky as if to check the weather. He then sniffed the air with a quick snort. "I must find Rhom." Terth was now in the hands of the Jamtori. He would find his answers there. He thought.

The seasoned veteran checked the straps of his monsu and tonsu. Next, he secured the buckles on the upper portion of his harness. Covering it all was a short leaf patterned poncho. He silently alighted on a lower branch above him. Brawzen paused for a quick look at the now empty home that had been his from birth, empty with no family left to bring life to those aging walls. Turning his gaze north, Brawzen leaped out and into the foliage with a slight rustle of leaves and was gone.

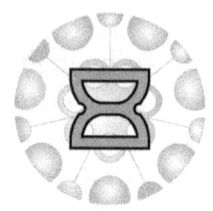

First light, the jindips were already busy broadcasting their proud "chit, chit" from the upper branches. Yereni quietly made her way to the larder for a few extra items before going out the back opening. It had been a week now and the collection of missing pilfered goods was sure to be noticed by her mother any day. Nevertheless, the secret she kept was worth the risk.

Quickly gearing up and checking her reflection in the well, she silently bound down the hill and away to see her new friend. Rhom was improving day by day. The cuts from the radoacs had healed nicely. His leg aside from a dark hole where the cornas had pierced him had regained much of its mobility. Yereni could tell he was getting antsy to leave. But she liked the company and hearing about the others in the Havens. Even the chores were not so bad right now. Better to get them done quickly and have more time to see Rhom. Approaching the platform, she could see he was awake. He stood along the outer rail watching the sun peek over the distant hills and its rays penetrate the nearer canopy. The misty air revealed blades of light spanning the forest openings, diffusing the beams into swirling fingers.

"Day's Begin to you, Yereni!" Rhom called down from the bower refuge.

"Forest's favor to you, Rhom!" she replied, climbing up the trunk toward the access hatch.

"Brought you some food. Some roasted plimpnuts, a fresh vineglobe, and a piece of my mom's sweet bread." Rhom smiled and sat down with her to share the meal. While they ate, Yereni, ever curious, started the conversation.

"What was it like for you and your friend when you were small? Did you get to play games with all the others? What kind of games do you play? What is that one I always see in the clearing? You know the one where one kid sits in the middle and the others run around the edge, leaping in and out with feathers in their hands?" The questions flew.

"Ah, you mean Flinter's Folly. We used to play that when we were little."

"Tell me about it, please Rhom." She looked at him wide-eyed. Rhom looked at her sitting there so expectantly. A quirky smile crossed his face. She reminded him of how Terth would get whenever they would ask Uncle Brawzen about his time in the Bellop Wars. Terth would never be satisfied. He was constantly probing his uncle for facts. Yereni was doing the same.

"Well, ok but it is really just a silly game," he began. "You start by picking a stone and a feather from a basket in the center of the clearing. Next, we would all take a turn tossing a stone at the upside-down basket. The one who ends up the farthest from the center is the Gromli and must sit in the middle of the clearing with a blindfold. Everyone else becomes Flinter. The goal is to get the

Gromli to lose focus and move. The better the resolve, the longer the Gromli can resist the feather onslaught."

"Oh, that is not what it looks like from the trees and doesn't sound fun at all. How does it end?" Yereni interjected.

"Well, there are two ways it can end. A good Gromli will surprise a Flinter, reach out, and snatch the feather even with the blindfold on. The other option, which more often is what happens, a Gromli will lose their focus, move, lash out, or miss grabbing a feather, which makes them out for the next couple of rounds. Most choose to go home or wander away to play with other younglings instead of waiting."

"That definitely doesn't sound like fun at all." Yereni was glad at that moment that she'd never been a Gromli. "Why play such an awful game?"

"I never thought of it as awful. Terth loved it and was always coercing the others to play. I guess I was just used to it. It's not that bad really, you just remain calm and try to let the hand of Jaru guide you. Terth was quick and would always get a feather. Me, I just sat facing the sun so I could 'feel' the shadows and do my best." Rhom shrugged as he finished his reply. "So, what do you think about me getting down from this place and heading back to the Havens? I need to check on my uncle and I'm sure Splicer's pet snifty has eaten all the shortleaf I set out to dry. I really need to get back."

"I'm not sure you are ready to go anywhere. That leg of yours looks kind of wobbly. The day feels like it is going to be hot, and I thought I saw another sortie of radoacs on the way here. Besides, you don't even have a harness or mon-tons to use." Yereni did her best to conceal the panic in her voice. She had found a friend of her own who could explain how the Crelli lived in the Havens. There were so many questions left, he couldn't leave yet.

"One day more. Ok?" She tried to show her best smile, the one she gave her dad whenever he was upset with her for skipping a chore.

"Ok, but tomorrow we head down the valley. You can even go with me. It will be fine. I'm sure Uncle Brawzen will enjoy the extra company with Terth gone."

"Rhom, tell me more about the Havens," she said, not wishing to think about tomorrow or what excuse she might need to create to keep him here for just one more day.

"**H**ave you been eating late-night snacks again? You know what happens when you eat like that. You end up tossing and turning all night and I am the one who doesn't get any sleep." Mallahen was flustered. This was the third batch of sweet bread in two weeks.

"Huh? Oh. It's not me." Bendohl was trying to focus on a new type of gearing to improve the control unit on a monsu module, and this was not the time to discuss sweet bread. "Check with that flaptorious daughter of ours."

"I would, but she is never around when I think to ask." Mallahen continued, "I hear her get up early but by the time I get in the common room, she is out the back door. When she returns, it's been such a long day, I forget to bring it up. Why only this morning I barely got a 'Bye Mumma' from her as she went out." Mallahen made an internal note "Tonight I will mark the jars, and in the morning, I will get up early and just see if she is the one."

"Well, she has been collecting soil and plant samples for me at a tremendous rate. Maybe the extra food is giving her extra energy." Bendohl's reply was an attempt to end the discussion.

The afternoon pressed on. Bendohl was, as always, tinkering with some apparatus or other. He occupied his evenings with mapping soil samples and coordinating the next day's location. Years before, he had sustained an injury to his lower back. This caused his right leg to remain in a half-cocked position and locked at his hip. He could travel by ground, but traversing the branch highways of the upper canopy was out of the question and Crelli don't travel the forest floor unless in large number. Bendohl counted on his daughter to provide him with the information he needed. Both Yereni and Mallahen knew better than to impede his work.

As eccentric as Bendohl was, the withdrawal from influence by his peers provided undivided attention to his theories. His focus centralized around the cradle of life found in the valley. Why did growth halt at the ridgeline surrounding the edges? It was strange how the vegetation and wildlife rapidly dissipated the farther one traveled from the valley, especially north.

The sky was violet. The moon was in its dark phase. A few stars were visible between the trees above. Yereni arrived home quietly. She entered the rear door and descended a ramp to a long, low substructure below their home. Silently, she opened the door just in time to see her father close the lid on a round drum-shaped case and cover it with a tarp. A light on the top turned from blue to red as he turned a sunken handle clockwise. Her eyes flashed slightly as curious thoughts crossed her mind. Bendohl turned around in time to catch the last ray in her eye and reveal the defensive thoughts in his. The two shared what seemed to be a century-long awkward moment.

"So, child, what did you find today?" he asked.

"Well, the flowers along the south slopes are continuing to spread downstream," Yereni said. "I saw color variations not noted before. I brought samples of each new shade. Also, I found one with nine petals instead of eight."

"Excellent, my dear, now leave everything on the tables." Bendohl hooked his arm in hers and turned her away from the far wall and the container. He continued, "Tomorrow, I want you to take a trip to the falls on the Vigrop border near Two Rocks. You know, the ones leaning on each other like tired fighters."

"Yes, Poppa," she replied, casting a last glance over her shoulder at the container as she made her exit through the door and up the ramp.

Making her way through the communal area, she peeked into her parents' room to see if her mother was awake. Mallahen was gently breathing with closed eyes. Satisfied with her mom's status, Yereni climbed a set of bars sticking out from the trunk of the tree their home was anchored to.

The majority of Crelli buildings were elevated about 15-20 feet above ground with a platform surrounding the trunk of a large tree. Sometimes, a larger structure might span multiple trees. An average home would consist of a main platform with a larger donut-shaped room wrapping the tree. Individual rooms would be built on crescent-shaped platforms either above or below the main. Covered tunnels would connect these additional rooms with hatches on the ends. Some ladders might be vertical, but others would ascend or descend at other angles following the curve on the tree. In Yereni's instance, the tunnel was at a thirty degree angle from the plain with metal bars spaced out to assist the climber.

Opening the hatch, she crawled in and lay down

on a pile of blankets woven by the nimble hands of the Vigrop. With the change created by the Jambat/Visatae came a new but wary peace with the Vigrop. Peddlers could be found traveling the border areas. It was becoming more common for Crelli to trade baked goods and cured fruits for the tools and finer textiles the Vigrop could produce. Yereni had traded her meal for these blankets some months ago. Proudly coming home with her prize, her father chastised her for contacting this "forest rabble," as he put it. Nevertheless, she liked the blankets, and they were hers. Since her father's injury, he didn't attempt to climb to her room, and the blankets were a forgotten topic along with other various treasures she had collected.

Curling up in the center, she leaned out to turn a crank, opening a slotted vent in the roof, which looked like a tub drain or flour sifter, to allow a cooling breeze to waft about the room. She thought about the day she had spent with Rhom. It was now almost two months and his thoughts about returning to the village had waned. The outpost was his home, and she was a daily visitor. He began to fish, hunt fruit, and scout early in the mornings before she arrived. Borrowing from her mother's stock, she would prepare whatever he brought back.

Afterward, they would go out together to the remote regions to collect the samples. Yereni was still cautious and would avoid bringing him along to any regions where Crelli lived. She didn't want to lose her special friend—her only friend. On those days, she would think of some quest for him or a long task to occupy time. Of course, she would always offer a reward to inspire him to accept, mostly sweet bread. Once the day's work was done, they would lie on their backs on the outpost's platform and talk about whatever came to mind, meaning mostly she would ask questions and Rhom would be expected to give answers.

A smile crossed Yereni's face until she remembered the case in her father's workshop. What was in it? Her smile faded as her brow furrowed. She had never seen it in her father's workshop before, and why did he look so nervous? Where did it come from and who did it belong to? She drifted off to sleep, considering the container and its purpose. The enigma had worn her out.

Meanwhile, a comfortable and slightly sleepy Rhomazel was contemplating his dilemmas. That vision he had of his mother seemed genuine enough. He could recall the location clearly. Even after the past two months the conversation, too, was memorable. She had told him he was not alone and now he had a new friend, someone other than Terth. Yereni was fun and adventurous, not to mention she was attractive as well. He loved the way she would laugh; it was an awkward giggle with an occasional tiny snort, but it was genuine, and he liked it.

His wounds were healed, and he had a place to stay, company, and food. What more did he need? He didn't want to go back to the Havens. Part of him didn't want to face Brawzen and accept what he had told him. The other part didn't want to see Terth now that he was in the Jamtori and Rhom was not.

Rhom always felt like the lesser of the two of them, and the current situation did not help matters. No, he was fine right here for now. So why did he feel restless at night, especially when the moon was close and in full view? It was like the moon now had a face of its own. It stood there high above him in silent judgment. Rhom would avoid the sight of it at night. Perhaps his mother would visit him again and help him with the answers. "Sleep then. Sleep might bring her to me."

———————

Early the next morning, Yereni crept into the cooking area, as had been the new daily habit for some time now. "Perhaps Rhom will have a fish from the stream." Making sure not to forget the sweet bread, she went out the back and away into the trees. Unknown to Yereni, a silent shadow appeared from below the home's platform and a figure leaped into the trees behind her.

Rhom was standing on the platform, happy to see the misty morning. He heard the rustle of the branches from the south and knew Yereni was close. He waved as she alighted on the platform.

"Did you fish this morning?" she asked.

"As a matter of fact, yes." He lifted a long red fish into the air with a sideways smile on his face.

"Well then, it's good I brought these," She said, revealing a cloth full of fresh herbs and spices, along with two vegetables like onions.

"I will get the fire up! I can't wait to eat this giant whopper of a fish I caught!" Rhom said.

Both were so preoccupied that neither noticed the lone figure standing behind them. A voice bellowed out.

"So, is this what happened to all my sweet bread? Who are you, and how dare you coerce my daughter into stealing for you? Yereni, get behind me now. You don't even know who he is or what he is capable of. Has he hurt you in any way?" Mallahen was angry.

"Mumma, it is not like that; Rhom is kind, and he

is my friend."

"Ma'am, I assure you I have done nothing wrong. We're just friends. Sh-sh-she helped me when I was injured. I'm from the Havens. I'm just a kid." Rhom was trying his best to be earnest. An angry Crelli mother was not to be trifled with. Not having experience with mothers, they all intimidated him a bit.

"Why are you out here? Who sent you? What is your name? Are you with the council? Did the Jamtori send you?" Mallahen was furious. With so many questions, Rhom's head was spinning. Suddenly, they all heard a low hiss. Turning around, the three of them were looking directly into a group of about eight Vigrop with nets and leashes in hand.

Picking up the closest object which happened to be the cooking pan, Rhom leaped in front of Yereni and her mother. "Get behind me. I'll protect you."

"You're just a pup," Mallahen said. She was armed with an older monsu and tonsu similar in design to that of Yereni's. Stepping past Rhom, she engaged in close combat with the two Vigrop on the right side of the room. Taking her cue from her mother, Yereni adopted a defensive stance to the left of Rhom. Looking from mother to daughter and then to the frying pan, Rhom gave his best yell. Charging forward, he swung the pan above his head, attempting to hammer it down on the head of his closest opponent.

The lizard was not in danger. Lifting his hands, he threw a net toward Rhom, ensnaring him. A second Vigrop tossed a lasso over the net, cinching it down tightly across Rhom's waist. He was stuck, the pan still in his hand.

Yereni was doing her best to hold her own. Moving in close, she used her monsu expertly. She gave a quick block to the right, followed by a fast uppercut with the left. A knee to the stomach of the lizard in front of her followed by a full-legged sweep behind her with tonsu extended. The explosive kick slashed the Vigrop standing behind her full across the upper leg. He dropped his leash and howled out in pain. Mallahen was faring even better. Her first two opponents were on the ground out for the count. The trapped Rhom was amazed. "Who are these women?" he thought. No longer a threat, the two Vigrop who had captured Rhom turned to assist the others.

A smaller Vigrop had managed to get a rope around Yereni's ankle. He was doing his best to pull her down. Annoyed, she tried to swing her left arm down to cut the rope with the tip of her monsu. At that moment, it tossed a net over her from behind and to the right. Struggling against the net, two more ropes sailed out and over her head. Yereni was caught.

Mallahen, seeing her daughter struggle, intensified her attack. Taking out two more lizards, she turned to face the remaining four. The smallest one let out a loud clicking whistle sound. Below, the tree vibrated. The thud-thud of feet, large heavy feet, on the platform drew closer. A large Bellop entered wearing a pair of dreaded "Heavy Hands," a thick bar of metal over the top of the fingers like brass knuckles only thicker and wider. Reaching out, he grabbed the table and tossed it at Mallahen. Lifting her arms and crossing them, she did her best to deflect the heavy object. This was the distraction the Vigrop needed. Ropes flew out from all four. It was too late. They ensnared as well Mallahen.

The beastly Bellop waded across the room, brushing furniture, supplies, and debris aside. Reaching out and grasping her by the neck, he effortlessly lifted Mallahen. The Vigrop backed off, hissing. The hulking creature opened his mouth and the horns on either side of his face spread wide as he did. The beast let out a mighty roar. The air shook from the sound. Rhom and Yereni starred in horror and disbelief as the jaws of the mighty Bellop clamped down across the back of Mallahen's neck. The crunch and crack of her spine shattering could be heard throughout the room. A gasp of air fled her throat as her body went limp. Yereni screamed out as the monster tore away at her mother's neck. Overcome by the shock, Rhom froze. The Vigrop in the room cowered away from the beast, not wanting to be mistaken as the next target.

Dragging his meal across the room the Bellop exited the building to consume alone. Yereni fought her restraints. The flood of rage washing over her body was too much for the captors. Seeing her movements, Rhom gathered his senses. Looking down, he could see a short dagger on the belt of an unconscious Vigrop to his right. Extending his leg, he loosened it with his foot. Rhom let his body go limp and fell to the ground. The continued commotion caused by the enraged and grieving Yereni distracted the Vigrop crew. Rhom felt around behind, searching for the pommel of the dagger. Fumbling for what seemed an eternity, Rhom grabbed hold of the handle. Flipping the blade upward, he sawed against the rope until it snapped. Looking up, Rhom could see Yereni's face. Tears streamed down as she roared out in pain. Her eyes were wide, her nostrils flared, and foam collected at the corners of her mouth.

A faint blue glow appeared around the edges of her harness. The light intensified as small crackles of light raced across the edges of her equipment. Fingers of electricity speared out around her, connecting to objects around the room. The Vigrop recoiled in fear. Rhom could feel his hair standing on edge as the air was alive with energy. The ropes around Yereni slacked as she lifted her hands. Rhom ducked behind a storage locker as the ball of blue energy blasted out and away from Yereni in every direction. The Vigrop attackers sailed across the room. Bolts of energy licked around the locker and pricked the skin along Rhom's exposed areas. As the energy penetrated him, Rhom heard Yereni. He could hear her scream. Not just the scream in the air, he heard the scream in his mind. He felt her, the emotions, the pain, the vision of her mother. The audible and inner screams were slightly off, causing a delay so minor it was almost stereo. Rhom couldn't bear it. The flow of data was too much. The energy pulsing through his body was painful. He yelled out.

"Stop!" she heard. Yereni couldn't. Her body was not her own. A surge of emotions, along with something else, was building inside her chest. Every part of her was alive. The ends of her fingers were crackling with blue flames. Her hair was on end, muscles taut and frozen in place. Again, she heard it. "Stop!"

This time, it was louder. Her eyes opened. The explosion of energy around the room was coming from her. A second group of Vigrop entered the room. The leader pulled a pair of smooth metal balls from his pouch. Swinging his arm above his head, he let them go. A slender line attached to the two spheres twirled through the air toward Yereni. His aim was true. The rope wrapped tightly around her neck. One ball, in its final rotation struck her squarely on the side of the head and she was knocked to the ground, unconscious. The blue bolts of energy stopped. Yereni was caught, and the other intruders made short work of Rhom, tying fresh restraints around him. It was over. Yereni's mother was no more, and they were captured.

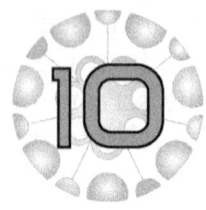

10

Moving silently across the bowers high above the forest floor, a group of shadowed figures made their way east across the valley. The smooth swoosh sound of monsu sliding in and out was rhythmic and in sync. The team was young and newly formed. It was rare to see a class of Jambat develop a cadence as quickly as this last batch had done. Leading the group through the night's exercise was taking all of Raunt's skills. They were swift and agile. The foresight given to them by the Visatae was in full use. Reaching a large clearing, Raunt stopped short of the edge and paused a moment for the group to take formation along the perimeter. Clearing his mind, he could sense the actions of the others. Like faint, glowing silhouettes of varying colors, he could envision Terth and his team.

Below them, in the clearing, a group of Bellop nomads had just finished feasting on their latest meal of ransacked and pillaged goods from Crelli storehouses. The large-scale battles of The Great War may have been over, but the Crelli had a long way to go in securing their land against the Bellop. Terth sensed his team was ready.

Looking across the clearing, he could see the glow coming from Old Raunt. Everything was in place. On cue, Valden the Jambat to the left of Terth dropped to the ground in front of the pile of nomad Bellop.

"Evening boys," he cheerfully said. "Time to pay the tab!"

Looking up from their meal, a couple of them grunted. A larger beast with a long patch of furless skin along his neck waved an arm toward Valden dismissively. Moori and Sheidel leaped down from the trees on the opposite side of the pack, and another Bellop stood to his feet. Lifting his head to the sky, the enormous brute cursed the heavens with a tremendous roar. Chaos exploded in the clearing. The Bellop group, numbering between fifteen and twenty, spread out around the clearing in search of the nearest target. The remaining Jambat team members descended upon the grassy floor. Fully equipped with monsu, tonsu, and padded half-suits, the group was ready to engage the Bellop. Eyeing the equipment and increased number of opponents, the nomads hesitated.

Terth felt a shift in the air and a slight change in hue around Craznak to his left. He was the strongest of their group but was headstrong and brash. Terth charged toward him, reaching out with his right arm toward the open and ready grasp of his large friend Craznak. He clasped his hands firmly together, creating a cradle for Terth to handspring. Terth was launched into the air. Gracefully twisting, he landed squarely on the back of a surprised Bellop. Extending his monsu to full length, he pierced the sides of the beast under the arms and through the ribcage. The blow was so deep the tips emerged from the skin above the stomach on the other side of the creature. Howling in pain as life seeped from the open wounds, the cry ended in gurgles as his body proceeded to slump.

Leaping away in a backflip, Terth landed a few feet behind, just as another Bellop charged across the area toward Craznak. Smiling at the challenge, he took a wide, balanced stance to face his opponent head-on. The Bellop was equipped with a rectangular forearm buckler. Craznak went limp, falling to the ground as the beast charged over him. Kicking his feet up, he inserted both tonsu into the chest of the Bellop; he pushed off the ground with the additional force of his monsu. Landing a few feet away, Craznak grunted in satisfaction at his maneuver.

The battle in the clearing was over quickly. The team had exacted their judgment flawlessly. Landing in the center of the team Raunt called out.

"Status report."

"Area secure, patrol group fifty-two intact," was the response from the team in unison.

"Let's get these stores secure. Craznak, you and Terth pile the Bellop on the far side. Moori, take Berendi and alert the citadel to send a group to collect the supplies. Delpar and Sheidel, go topside and stand watch." Raunt's directions were obeyed quickly with silence. A chill went up his spine as he watched the precision of this team. Even Valden had taken the cue and was quickly rescuing the supply containers. No team he could remember was this controlled. No doubt about it, this patrol was something special.

Preparing to respond to Raunt's order, the team froze. Something was wrong. The group tensed. Moori and Berendi froze at the far end of the clearing. Raunt reached out to the group, signaling to regroup to standard tactical positions. Silently, the group slid into place. Along the clearing edge to the east, the team could detect a mass of figures, but their halos were obscured. Rows of large

Bellop stepped from the shadows. Clothed in a dark red and gray jerkin, they blended with the background. The weapons they carried were dulled with pitch. Not only did this group of Bellop appear different, but the calm demeanor was also unusual. The new opponent wore a harness and pouch. The Bellop stood in unison. A smaller figure made its way from the shadows to stand in front. It was a Vigrop dressed similar to the Bellop task force.

"Skelkiz," Raunt uttered, clearly shaken by the appearance of this new arrival. "What abomination have you created this time?"

"Why should the Crelli be the only ones to receive the Blessing of Jaru? The Visatae are for all," Skelkiz replied.

Terth tried extending his senses, only to find nothing. It was as if the new group absorbed his energy. No wonder they weren't detected before.

The rest of patrol fifty-two fared no better. Even their local connection was muffled.

"What is this mockery, you slinking worm?" Raunt's voice was taut as he yelled across the clearing.

The lizard grinned. As he barred his teeth, a dark tongue flicked out. His eyes gleamed as his focus centered on Raunt. "I dug deep. Just like they commanded; 'Dig deep Skelkiz, find us more' they would say to us. So, we dig deep, yes, very deep. Find new eggs the Vigrop did." You could see the pleasure on his face, so proud of his accomplishment. He continued, "The Remplancant was much pleased with us. Reward us she did. Gave us our own army."

Terth noticed Skelkiz had an odd harness. It looked less like leather and more like dark, shiny blue bone. Then he saw it. A large pair of wings flicked along his back. It was not a harness, but legs wrapped around his waist and

67

shoulders. A large, round mouth was sealed to the back of his neck.

The Vigrop extended his arms wide. "Oh yes, we can sense you, young Crelli. We are the Visatae Dobai. You are strong, but we can make you powerful."

"Enough!" Raunt shouted. "We are Jamtori! Team, execute Shatterstone now." The group floundered the formation. Tightening up in a small circle, they stood their ground as the Bellop advanced. The Visatae, normally ready to assist, were stolid. Terth was distracted, still considering the comments of Skelkiz.

"Did he sense my thoughts?" Terth was stuck, frozen by his doubt. Large nets were hurled over Patrol fifty-two. They were trapped. The Visatae had failed them. Nothing like this had ever happened before.

Skelkiz sneered, "Dig deep, Crelli. Now you will dig deep."

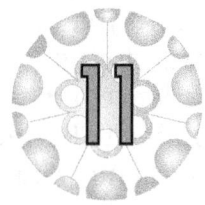

The morning mist swirled among the branches, passing through the canopy, rising toward the open sky, to wisp away with the breeze. Brawzen looked down from a tall branch at the clearing. Something major had happened here. Dropping to the platform, he could detect a burnt smell even before he entered the outpost. The furniture was broken and in disarray. Dark, dried blood spread in every direction. Black marks zagged across the room, starting from the far wall.

He made his way down the platform hatch to the ground, then circled the base of the tree. A pile of torn clothes, now rags, flapped in the breeze. Brawzen could tell they were Crelli-made. The remains were a jumbled mass of flesh and bone. The buzz of insects could be heard as he neared. Nature's cleaning crew was busy consuming the dried flesh. Turning back to the outpost, Brawzen gathered what loose wood he could find. He drove the ends of the wood into the dirt around the corpse. Next, he placed what stones he could find around the perimeter. Taking his firestones from his pack, he struck them together to create a spark. Gently blowing on the small embers at the end of a piece of dried moss, he soon had a small flame. As the flame grew, Brawzen recited a small verse.

"May Jaru guide you to your place of rest. May your family be swift to find you on the day of unification. Watch from high and wait for us."

He waited in silence for the fire to burn and eventually die out. Standing to his feet, Brawzen turned to the south. Leaping to the canopy, he exited the clearing. A few trails of blue-gray smoke rose to mix with the lighter, now midday mist of the leafy roof covering the area.

Whatever had happened in the clearing was recent, a few days at most. The marks in the grass revealed both Vigrop and Bellop were at the scene. Brawzen knew outcast groups would often band together, preying on unsuspecting Crelli. It was unusual for them to head this far west. What could be happening in the region? Brawzen had been away from the Havens a little more than a month. Famine, disease, overpopulation, political unrest, or crime, any one or combination could drive the desperate far from home, but he would have known about those. Whatever was fueling this group's courage was something different.

As Brawzen ran through the different scenarios, leading deeper into the endless trails of possibilities, he could hear a soft whizzing approaching. The sound, low at first, grew louder. The shiny glint of metal twinked in his eye as the day's light captured the moving object. The device slowed at the crest of a small hill. Brawzen slid back against the firm mast of the tree, allowing the leaves and shadows to conceal him.

The vehicle—Brawzen knew it was no beast—was not large. Four legs looking very much like tonsu could be seen at the edges. A single seat was suspended in the center between two "A'" shaped supports, and a bundle of cables converged along either side of the chair. The whizzing sound came from a small engine directly behind the seat. Coming to a halt, the noise died down. The driver—a Crelli—slid forward and out of the chair. Brawzen could see their right leg was impaired. The pilot turned to scan the area where he was stationed. A slight smile crossed Brawzen's face.

Descending the tree along the shadowed side, he made his way around the edge of the clearing toward the vehicle and driver. Careful to remain hidden, Brawzen, the veteran forest protector, used his recently revived skills to silently approach the apparatus from the rear. The driver, intent on scanning the clearing, was gripping a long, thin spear to maintain his balance.

"Care to tell me what this unholy contraption is called, Brimble?" Brawzen called out as he approached the vehicle. The surprised Bendohl stumbled, rolled, and popped up to face Brawzen.

"C'mon now Bumble, I seem to recall your combat skills are nowhere near mine," Brawzen said while brushing aside the spear tip with his left hand and extending his right in friendship.

"Trust you to mess up my name, Brawzen, you big bully," Bendohl gruffly replied. He took the hand, nonetheless. Straightening his garments and fluffing the dust from his hair, he greeted the Crelli openly.

"What are you doing out in the forest with this whirring beast?" Brawzen said, clapping a metal leg on the machine with a thud.

"I am looking for my family, so if you are not going to help me, then I must be on my way." Bendohl was taxed.

"Family?" Brawzen thought instantly to the outpost

across the way and the poor soul put to rest below. "What has happened? When did you last see them?"

"Five days. It has been five days. I woke to silence. The house was empty. I called out, but no response came. At first, I thought the two of them were merely out, as it was still morning. Time passed, and I grew worried." Bendohl's weak leg quivered as he stood there. Brawzen pointed to the seat in the walker and helped Bendohl into the chair. He continued his story. "I made my way to the outside of the compound and called out. Again, no reply came. Fearing something terrible, I secured the lab and house. I grabbed the few things I could see that I might need and began my search. I have been making circles spiraling from the house, returning each night."

"Bendohl, I must tell you. Across the clearing is an old Crelli outpost. Just this morning I was there. A fierce battle recently took place. I could see scorch marks all along the inside walls. And... and... something else, I found remains, mostly Vigrop, but there was a Crelli, at least one." As soon as Brawzen said Crelli, Bendohl slammed his steed into gear and whizzed off toward the far end of the clearing.

Racing full speed, he reached the base of the tree. Making his way around Bendohl found the charred remnants of the bier. Looking down at the still-warm ashes, he spied a blackened curved piece of metal. He recognized it at once. It was the twisted, broken centerpiece of a bracelet Mallahen wore. Bendohl's thoughts raced. The shadowed chains of "what if's" smothered him. His injury, his focus on his experiments, his gruff dismissive manner, the forest, the Bellop, even Jaru, everything was to blame. His thoughts spiraled down a darkening hole.

Brawzen rounded the corner to see the huddled form of Bendohl examining the keepsake. The heavy thoughts Bendohl was experiencing could be felt through the air. Brawzen took a seat on a smooth stone a few yards away. "Better to let him be than shake the hive," Brawzen thought.

Brawzen opened his eyes. The colors around the clearing had shifted, meaning the sun would set soon. He had dozed off. Tersely planting his feet and leaning forward to scan the area, he noticed Bendohl was gone. Turning his headfirst to the left and then right, he listened for anything unusual. A shuffling sound could be heard on the far side of the tree. Rounding the enormous trunk, Brawzen looked up to see a struggling Bendohl making his best effort to ascend a hooked rope to the Outpost platform.

"What are you doing?" Brawzen called out.

"I have to see," Bendohl replied. "I need to know about... about Yereni." The struggle to climb the rope combined with his broken spirit and shaken nerves was wrenching to watch. Brawzen offered to assist. The two of them reached the platform and entered the shambled room. Flipping over containers and brushing aside debris, Bendohl scoured the room for some sign, any sign of his daughter. Behind the over-ended table, he found Yereni's sling bag still full of raided items from the kitchen. Aside from a few exposed nibbled and hardening ends, the sealed items were intact.

"Brawzen, I need you to help me." The look on Bendohl's face was grave. "I don't know why you are out here or what happened to the two you were responsible for. What I do know is you are here now, and clearly Jaru has destined this meeting. Actions are being taken even now to upend all that we are as Crelli." He paused for a moment to study Brawzen. "If you don't help me now, life for all Crellantan will be horribly changed forever."

Rhom awoke to darkness. His hands and feet were bound, and he was lying on his side. The area was small, and he could not fully stretch his body. A shroud covered his eyes. But Crelli have other senses. He sniffed. The air smelled wet and dank. His skin felt warm. He could hear a trickling sound. Water was nearby and beyond, faint voices. The sound of the conversation grew louder.

"I lost quite a few today and will need compensation," the first voice uttered. The dialect was Vigrop.

"You will be rewarded. Skelkiz does not forget the faithful," the second replied.

Rhom leveled his breathing and remained motionless. The sound of moving fabric and footsteps paused.

"Is this the one?" the second voice asked.

"She caused us much trouble, but we are not weak. No, we are strong. We took her," the first voice replied boastfully.

"You are certain she is a Strand?" said the second voice.

"Look at the burns on my arms. The blue fire did this. Many credits are owed to us. The marks will not go away soon."

Rhom was now certain Yereni was nearby. Alive for sure, but in what condition he did not know.

"What about the other one?" The second voice said this while giving a sharp clang to the side of the cell. The entombed Rhom felt the engulfing vibration.

"He is a mere pup, easily taken. He did not even see the ropes. This one knows nothing." The voice was that of the leader of the group who had taken them from the outpost. The assessment of his skills bothered Rhom.

"I wasn't even armed like the others," he thought. "That thing that happened with Yereni was hurting everyone, even me."

Thinking back to the moments of pain and confusion in that room, a fleeting thought crossed his mind. There was a point where he had traded places with her. He was in her mind. The pain was horrible then, but now he had the memory. Reviewing the experience, Rhom was looking at her and he was looking at himself at the same time. An odd experience, no doubt. He remembered desperately trying to get her attention, but beyond that, whatever had caused this anomaly, he could not say.

"It doesn't matter. All Crelli under twenty seasons are to be taken to Skelkiz, even this one." The leader of the raiding party continued, "Now pay."

"Very well," the second voice replied, "But the slow one gets a regular rate. Your losses are your own, hunter."

"Varghhhzzz," the raid leader growled. Nothing else was to be done. The sound of the two Vigrop drifted away, leaving only the tinkling of dripping liquid from before. Rhom was cramped, hungry, and sore. The distraction of the voices had ended, and Rhom was alone. His thoughts turned inward, his body screaming for attention. The recent rolling rock of events life had thrown him into was taxing. A small ball of self-pity grew in his heart. He thought he was the unluckiest Crelli to live, with no family, no home, no friends. His list of negatives grew. The heaviness pressed him to sleep, a self-inflicted coma of woe.

Meanwhile, a very confused and heartbroken Yereni, who was listening to the same conversation not far from Rhom, was going through her recap of past events. The horrid vision of the Bellop stealing the life of her mother fueled the fierce fire of vengeance in her. Her muscles ached under the restraints. The darkness didn't help either. The red glow of aggress crept into her eyes. A dark sliver worked its way into her heart. Not only did she blame the Bellop. She blamed the Vigrop, the forest, part of her even accused Rhom. Why did he not fight harder?

What had happened in that room? Yereni knew about power sources from her father's experiments, but there was nothing in the outpost capable of projecting energy like what she saw. Her back had been to the wall, no devices were behind her. Had the Vigrop developed something new? Is that what was in the case her father was hiding? Beyond that, she recalled the strange experience of hearing Rhom, stupid unhelpful Rhom, in her head, but he was across the room. The entire day was so wrong, it just made her angrier. Yereni waited like a coiled viper for her moment to spring at the first creature.

Sometime later, time enough had passed for Rhom to know he was beyond hungry, that place where thirst was greater than food. His lips were cracked, and his tongue was sticking to the rear of his mouth. His bound hands and feet were numb and cold. His elbows and knees ached in pain. The side of his hip was sore from the hard floor of his prison. Footsteps could be heard approaching the area again. The squeaking of pulleys and whizzing of cables was obvious. Whoever was out there was preparing to move the containers. Rhom listened attentively to the movements of the captors. The number of containers was up to nine by the time they got to his box.

The sound of doors swinging open was next. Rhom awaited his turn. He heard a sliding of metal and felt a slight change in the air and temperature above his head.

"Here you go, scum!" a rough voice said. A tube was shoved into the side of his dry, sore mouth. Something was being poured into his mouth. The warm liquid was bitter and smelled like old-cut grass with a hint of mushroom and soap. The thick fluid was repulsive, but the exhausted Crelli held it down as best he could. The door shut again, leaving Rhom in a teetering state of swallow or hurl, not sure of which would benefit him more.

Unknown hours passed as the prisoner caravan plodded along. Yereni could tell by the rigid corrections the cart made, they were on a track of some kind. The sounds from the wheels occasionally faded in and out. She determined they were traveling in a tunnel underground. The quieter areas must be open cavern areas where the walls were not so close. The jarring motion of the track did nothing to abate the pain in her body, nor did it aid her already fuming state of rage. Her anger had caused her to reject the abhorrent liquid they had tried to force down her throat, an action for which she now had second thoughts. Yereni was losing her strength. She had trouble thinking clearly and was facing difficulty staying awake.

Meanwhile, not far away, Rhom discovered the cart he was riding in had an odd shape on one wheel. The slight rocking motion of the imperfection once noticed was difficult to ignore. He began counting the time between wobbles. Once he figured out what the average was, he started counting the rotation of the wheel. Rhom was now over four thousand. Wherever they were headed was far from home.

He did the calculations in his head. It must have been about half a day since they left the area where the Vigrop had discussed the sale of Crelli. Rhom was still indignant about their assessment of his "abilities." They had only stopped once; the taste of the soapy soup came back the moment he thought of it. To counter the memory, he tried to recall the best meals of his past. At first, he thought about the meals with Yereni, quiet and pleasant for sure, but the recent tragedy and their current situation tainted those memories. He had to go further back to find a peaceful place.

For the first time in days, Rhom thought of Terth. He wondered how the training was going. Part of him was ashamed of running out on Uncle Brawzen. He had intended to go back but the attack by the cornas, his injuries, the new friendship with Yereni, and finally being captured by the Vigrop marauders was so much it felt like ages since he had seen either of them.

A strong jolt to the cart brought him back to his current situation. The motion had stopped. He could hear the screech of sliding metal and the clank of doors opening along the crates in the train. Rhom felt the change in the air as his cage was opened. A pair of cold hands pulled him out feet first. His equilibrium was off from the hours of cramped containment. The muscles in his legs were stiff and his head was swooning. The air was thick, dusty, and stale. The hood was removed from his head, revealing nothing. A pair of bright lamps blinded his vision, his eyes teared over. Instinctively, he looked down and away. A knock on his shoulder came from the jailer.

"Forward, rat," a voice spoke behind him. The blow made him stumble ahead a few feet. He tripped over a rock and fell forward, slamming his face into the ground. A rod was shoved between his bound arms, lifting him. The pain in his shoulders was immense. The jailer pushed him toward the collected group of captives huddled together a short distance away. Rhom spied Yereni in the group. Their eyes met for a moment. The connection was intense. He could sense her rage. The stone wall in her gaze reflected his pathetic attempt to connect. The emotional dagger hit him hard. The dejected Rhom lowered his eyes and found a place among the others.

B rawzen and Bendohl neared the compound just as the last ray of light cut across the ridgeline. Bendohl hopped from his vehicle and hobbled to the entrance. Brawzen followed. Once inside, he quickly secured the door as the two made their way down to the lab. He could see Bendohl fidgeting with a long cylinder underneath a tan tarp.

"I am about to show you something of immense importance. I do not yet know the full extent of the impact this discovery may have, but I do know it has the potential to change the balance of power in this region drastically." Bendohl stared directly at Brawzen to discern his intentions as he spoke.

"Inside this container is the future of the Visatae."

As he spoke Bendohl tapped a few buttons on the top of the cylinder. The center of the can rose from the outer sleeve, accompanied by a low hiss. Gentle wafts of vapor rolled out the sides and billowed to the floor. The inner tube was clear, providing an easy view of the contents. Brawzen gazed into the cylinder. It was a Visatae but not like any he had seen before. This specimen had legs and wings.

"Has it evolved? I knew something had been happening. The Rookery has been too quiet." Brawzen's mind raced as he spoke.

"Think back to what we know about Visatae, my friend." Bendohl closed the cylinder again and sat back in his lab chair.

"We know nothing. The Visatae are a mystery. We Crelli found eggs many years ago. Those eggs first came to the shore of the lake. Since then, Crelli teams have scoured the shoreline and the island at the center for more eggs. We store them in the Rookery, ready for the next team. We manage to locate a few each season, always just enough to start a new group of Jamtori. What happens to the Crelli when all the eggs are gone?"

"If that time comes, we fight as we always do," Brawzen replied.

"Yes, we fight, we fight until all the Jamtori are gone and the Bellop eat us all. No Visatae, no Jamtori, no Crelli. Don't you see? We must adapt again. Everyone keeps searching the surface of the lake, but what about the cliffs? What is buried there?"

Brawzen's brow furrowed as he listened.

Bendohl continued, "Some time ago, I encountered a group of Vigrop who had been fleeing their homeland. A team of Bellop pursued them across the hillsides. Eventually, they caught them and killed them all. The Vigrop fought for their lives to the end." He took a deep breath, "I observed their movements for several days before the final encounter and noticed some strange activity amongst the Vigrop the second night. Once I was sure the area was clear, I moved to figure things out for myself. That is when I found this container, along with information, very vital information. Do you know this specimen represents the next level in Visatae awareness? A more advanced form, capable of greater feats in combat, including flight. All the years of testing and prodding and dreaming in the Lab mean nothing compared to this."

"I thought you had forsaken that terrible work; think of the friends we lost."

"The minor loss of life is nothing if we are to preserve our species," Bendohl replied. "If we don't act, there will be no Crelli."

"At the cost of what? The Havens, the Crelli, our future?" Brawzen's voice quaked with emotion.

"Yes, the future. I was getting to that. You and a few of the council may know Stranded exist. I am the only one left who retains any scientific knowledge of what happened before the accident in the Lab. I have recovered a portion of the list and I will gather them together. A new type of Jamtori will be formed, capable of tremendous feats. Peace will come to all, peace under the new order of Crelli. An order commanded by me. We will remove the Visatae and control the vespridium."

"This is madness. What about Mallahen's daughter? Where is she? Shouldn't you be out looking for her?" Brawzen's anger was surfacing. His leg bounced and shook as he spoke.

"All in suitable time, my friend. It is true I had lost some hope. Her willfulness has been a barrier to what had originally been planned, but since this discovery, my fervor has been rekindled. From the burn marks at the outpost, something must have happened. Her strand mutation must have emerged, and I need to be there to kindle its development. Something has awakened the silent transposons, perhaps an adrenal or chemical release from stress. Some sort of L1 transcript has bridged the siRNA silencing mechanisms. I must find her and evaluate her blood. It was an unfortunate accident indeed, and I am saddened by the loss of Mallahen. However, the importance of this mission is far greater."

"Tell that to the poor girl! Tell her and see how she responds. She thinks you are her father! The greater good indeed—you were peculiar before the experiments and now that you have returned to them...you're twisted. The vespridium has driven you mad!" Brawzen rose to his feet preparing to attack. "The people need to know about this, or others will die like my sister. I can't let you leave with that container." Brawzen moved toward the cylinder. Bendohl flipped a switch along the underside of the chair arm. Several small tubes opened around the edge of the ceiling. Brawzen looked up at the nearest tube and then to Bendohl.

"I have to for the sake of Crellantan," Bendohl said, staring directly into the other's face. Smiling, he flipped a second switch. With a whoosh, thin metal darts blasted out of the opened tubes, burying themselves firmly into the hide of Brawzen. His body crumbled to the floor, motionless.

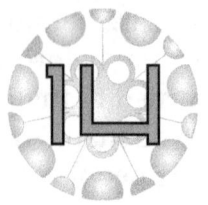

The moans of Crelli in pain and coughs from the dust filled the stale air. Beyond the opening and down the main bore, the incessant clang of tools on stone could faintly be heard. The overall din of sounds pressed a gray cloud upon Rhom and the other captives. He was exhausted. His arms ached. Miserable as he was, his companions in the shaft who had arrived before him were worse. Slumping down, he closed his eyes before the next round of work.

The days were a merry-go-round of consecutive changes. Each crew roused from rest in the pens would arrive at the excavation point of the tunnel. Then harnessed up, they began the task of pounding rock with monsu. These monsu were slightly modified, whereas the standard monsu would be tapered into a spike at the end. These were belled out beyond the fist into a pickaxe shape. Another group of diggers had monsu shaped like wedges. The wedge group would create fissures in the rock face, while the pickaxe group would weaken the cracks into rubble. The monsu were heavy and by the end of the first shift, the teams could barely lift their arms. A fresh team would change places and the crew would be off to the next shift.

After pounding rock for countless unknown hours, they herded the crews to a large room containing scores of large platforms straddling a long shaft. Teams would gather on each side of the shaft and press down on the platform. This would elevate the other side. The opposing crew would then, in turn press down on their side. The device was the source of power for everything in the shaft. The see-saw power of the bellows forced air down the shaft and expelled the foul used air. It also drove the gears of a large system of pulleys that towed the cars along the rail. Belts with exposed wooden teeth turned along one side of the rail and, by lowering a lever on the rail cart, you could engage the cart into the pulley system.

The final shift transitioned to the loading and unloading of cargo onto the rail cars. Crelli were poked and prodded into make-shift rows to pass loads of rubble onto carts or offloading timber to shore up the never-ending shaft.

Rhom had counted something close to thirty-five rest periods. Adding to the number of days he spent in recovery with Yereni, it was roughly one hundred days since he had been home. Nearly half a season! He missed Terth, Uncle Brawzen, and home, but mostly he missed Yereni. He was happy around her, however judging by the looks she gave him at their last parting, he doubted there would be another chance to enjoy time with her. He had not seen Yereni since the first day. The Vigrop had ushered her away with another female Crelli to some other unknown location. Since then, Rhom had searched the group, looking for a familiar face. Most of the Crelli housed with him were from other regions. His heart was empty. A gray slug of depression flowed through his veins.

This was his state the day Cloi showed up.

The large cell gate swung open and a group of a half dozen worn and beaten Crelli were flung into the center of the cave. A large Vigrop gave a stiff blow with a metal staff across the back of the last to enter. "Enjoy the rot, filthy tree vermin," he said as the large gate clanged shut. The new group collapsed in the center, all except one. She stood and faced the gate as if waiting for the Vigrop to return. Rhom recognized her at once. It was Cloi. She was the niece of old Raunt and although she was a few seasons older, Rhom and the others in his age group at the village knew her well. Cloi held all the records of achievement for just about every organized game the young played. Mysteriously, she had disappeared just before her time as a candidate for the Jamtori. No one in the Havens had heard from her since.

Rhom, with a dry, cracked voice, mustered up the words, "Cloi? Cloi, is that really you?"

With a quick turn of the head, she turned to face Rhom. "Who are you, and where did you hear that name?" The retort was sharp.

"I-I-I'm Rhomazel from the Havens. You know, I live with Brawzen near the Proving Grounds." He stammered through the last part, awkwardly considering his time away.

"Hmmph, a tawny runt of a scrub you were, though I see you have had your fair share of the world lately." It was true. His wounds had healed, but the scars were still there, the largest being the one on his leg, a present from the cornas.

"How did they catch you?" Rhom was full of questions.

"Not easily if that is what you are implying." She stood tall and proud as she said this. "Those horrible

86

Bellop were with them. Since when do Vigrop and Bellop openly hunt Crelli? Something is off. Why would they be so bold? It is our own fault, no doubt, always depending on those bugs to open our eyes when we need to be strong for ourselves."

Her comments reminded Rhom of what Brawzen had said in their last time together. She was the second person to recently show irreverence to the blessing of Jaru and the Visatae. "What do you know of the Visatae, Cloi?" The question was so openly stated. Rhom was determined to know more. Maybe there was another clue to be uprooted. He needed something to anchor to. The vision of his mother, the explosion of light at the outpost, the tragedy at the Lab, the story Uncle Brawzen had told him—something was missing. Maybe Cloi had a clue.

Looking directly at him, she made her face plain. "I am Cloi of the Havens. I am Crellan, a daughter of the forest, the land the True Provider gave us. I have sworn to protect my people from all threats from without and," she paused to look around the room, "and within." Her face had been plain, but the look in her eye gave Rhom hope.

The day dragged on longer than normal. An eternity passed before the tired crews were ushered once again into the holding blocks. Rhom had grown accustomed to the sour slop they were fed. That or he was just too tired to care anymore. Gulping down his portion, he soon made his way to the far side of the hollowed-out cavern. He slumped against the cold wall and drifted off into slumber.

A sharp flick to his ear awakened Rhom. Looking up, he could see the form of another Crelli leaning just beside him.

"So, young Rhomazel, tell me, what do you know of the Visatae?" Cloi peered at him intently.

"I don't know what I know anymore," he replied, looking down to break the power of her gaze.

"Well, that is a start. Perhaps you are smarter than you look." She relaxed just a little. Grabbing a thin rock, she rhythmically tapped the wall. "Do you know why I left the Havens?" She asked. "A few days before the hatching—the one I had been trained for, the one where I would most likely have been chosen for that abominable ritual—I was looking for something to wear to represent my mother, a bead, a jewel, a feather, anything to show that I was her daughter. My father had stowed her items soon after the event at the Labs. I only wanted the people to remember her, too. Searching through the containers deep below our tree, I found it—a box of my mother's belongings. There, right there on top, was a journal. I snatched it up, excited to read her words."

Cloi stopped for a moment, scanning the room. The others were all sound asleep. Taking a long breath, she sighed and resumed. "The experiments, testing done to our own people—it was unbelievable. I had seen my mother one way, but the person in this journal was unlike her in so many ways. I couldn't stop. I kept reading, searching for a glimpse of her intentions."

Rhom knew all too well the feelings she was describing. Looking up, he turned to face her again. "I know the truth about the Vespridium—it killed my mother." He could see Cloi's glassy eyes staring right back at him.

"Are you one too?" She scooted back slightly.

"What do you mean? One of what?" Rhom shifted his legs and leaned back. His eyes were wide and he had goosebumps all over.

"Tell me Rhomazel, what have you seen? Has anything out of the ordinary happened around you?"

Rhom all at once began a long splurt of emotions. He told Cloi all about his conversation with Uncle Brawzen, the events at the outpost with Yereni, and the blue flames, her voice in his head. He told her everything, though he decided not to say anything about his dreams and seeing his mother. It felt childish and too personal.

Far across the room, a body shifted slightly, an ear twitched and a pair of eyes opened just a slit.

"We can't stay here. We need to get back to my side of the forest. There is a group of Crelli you need to meet. Don't mention any of this here again. There are too many ears," Cloi said.

Right after watching Rhom be led away, Yereni was ushered from the railyard down a short tunnel and through a large room full of equipment. They crossed the room and exited into a long hallway full of doors. There were a couple of other Crelli with her. All of them were tied together in succession. The Vigrop would periodically stop and unshackle a few, placing each into their cell. Finally, it was Yereni's turn. The cell door was opened, and she was roughly pressed into the room from behind.

The door slammed shut behind her. Yereni turned and threw her whole body against the door in a fit of rage. That was the last of her energy. Sliding down, she slumped over and lay on the floor, exhausted.

Yereni woke with a jolt. A long, light robe had replaced her harness. The hem was lined with symbols. It reminded her of the writings she had seen in some of her father's journals. From the round bed she was on, she could see a washbasin in the corner with a small canister below for necessary functions. Otherwise, the room was clean and empty. The door slid open and a thin, tall Vigrop entered. He wore a harness with an apparatus mounted to the back which reminded her of the ones worn by Jamtori, only this one was larger. He gave a slight bow.

"I am Sssskelkizzzz, I will be your hossst until the director arrivessss." His tail gave a quick flick as he spoke. "I think you will enjoy your time with ussss. Yesssss enjoy."

Just as he finished, Yereni leaped from the bed and dashed for the open door. Crouching, she prepared to launch past Skelkiz and out the door to freedom. Forward, her body tumbled as she executed an aerial somersault slightly above and to the left of the Vigrop. A slight smile crossed her face as she sensed her body passing his. Then, in an instant, it was over. She felt a tight grip on her shoulder and another on her ankle. The room spun around as her body was slammed to the floor. The Vigrop jailer hovered over her. The room was filled with the hum of wings, the blur of which she could faintly see protruding from the back of Skelkiz.

"Not sssso fassst little one. We need you to ssstay HERE!" His tone spanned the spectrum from nice to gruesome in a flash. Her heart raced as she realized his grip had moved from her shoulder to her throat. His eyes glowed with a killing fever. A second later, his entire demeanor changed, and he resumed the appearance of a humble host. Skelkiz relaxed his grip, backed away, and brushed himself straight. The wings receded into slots along the container on his back, the tips peaking out below the bottom. "Now, I leave you to conssssider your actionssss. The nexssss time may prove to be more... ahhh...painful."

Yereni leaned forward on the end of the bed. "You won't get away with this. The next time might just be painful." She clenched her fists. "Painful for you!" So much anger remained from the death of her mother compiled with the fear she forced down. Her body quivered with unbridled emotion. The door closed, and the room was at once covered by a blanket of cold white silence.

A harsh voice woke Rhom, signaling once again time to get up, and the start of a new shift, for whatever that was worth. He stood, stretched, and panned the room. He could see Cloi across the way. Calm as ever, she walked to join the others in line. The day moved on like any other day. He felt sure Cloi would come to speak with him again after the meal, but she ignored him and he was too nervous to talk first. Rhom did not know anyone else in the room, nor did he trust anyone, either. Cloi was from his home, and he had hoped there was a chance for friendship.

The morning of the next shift and still no change. This went on for several days. It was as if the two had never spoken. Each shift Cloi would move away to join the team farthest from Rhom, ensuring their paths would not cross. Each meal she would blankly look across without acknowledging him.

Then one night Rhom awoke again to a sharp flick on the ear. "We have to move quickly; I think someone overheard us the last time." Cloi was face to face with Rhom. "Do you know how the bellows work?"

"Uhhuh" Rhom said.

"Yesterday, I noticed the main gear has a crack along a section of the teeth. It will break soon. When it does, the rail cars will be stopped and so will the flow of good air. The Vigrop will be focused on trying to get the repairs done. This will be our chance." She stopped and panned the room. Nothing stirred. "Just make sure you join my crew tomorrow." Without another word, Cloi backed away from Rhom and returned to the other side of the room.

The next shift, Rhom joined her crew which consisted of a dozen or so Crelli of various ages and in various states of health. Cloi donned a pair of heavy stone-breaker monsu and pounded the tunnel wall. Others braced the ceiling with timber, more for self-preservation than for the approval of the enslaving Vigrop engineers. Rhom grabbed a pair of long hand scoops and shoveled away at the rubble piling up below Cloi. He wanted so badly to talk, but knew it would just bring attention to them. What was her plan?

The shift changed, and they were now in the large room occupied by the bellows. Making their way down the rows of see-saw paddled platforms, Cloi gently moved the tired Crelli out of her way to the open slot nearest the large gear. Rhom did his best to keep up. He was able to get to the paddle group only one section away. Aside from the main opening from the shaft and the Crelli pens, the only other entrance was a small single door. Vigrop would enter and exit here during the day, and there were always two guards posted. Rhom scanned the room and counted. Fifteen Vigrop were on duty. He began to study the face of the Crelli in the room. Of the sixty working the bellows, maybe ten looked healthy enough to put up a fight.

One of the Crelli, weak from overwork and lack of

any nutrition, finally gave in to despair and melted into a crumbled pile of surrender. "SSSSanother one to feed to the bossssessss petsssss," sniggered the Vigrop penhold sentry overseeing the section of bellows near the large entrance. "You two get this pile of rot out of here." He motioned to a couple of underlings.

Cloi took advantage of the short distraction to pull a wedge of metal from her harness. It was the broken end of one of the monsu from the tunnel. Leaning over, she wedged it into the large main gear a few teeth back from the crack she had mentioned the night before. As the gear rotated, the wedge worked itself deeper, pushing the upper and lower cogs askew. A sharp squeal and the sound of metal bending quickly caught the attention of all around. The captives who had the wherewithal to perceive the situation pumped harder on the paddles, aggravating the tension on the main gear.

"Ssstop, ssstop, sstop!" An engineer rushed from the small door and toward the mechanism. The two guards ran behind him, leaving the door ajar. By now, everyone's attention was centered on the engineer running to the disturbance. Cloi stepped away and maneuvered toward the back of the crowd as she grabbed Rhom by the elbow and shuffled him along as well.

"This is working out better than I had hoped." She gave a quick smile as she spoke. "Are you ready?"

"I have nothing to lose," Rhom spoke as confidently as he could. Just as they were about to turn to make a sprint for the door, a short, pale Crelli with two missing teeth to the left of center stood directly in front of them.

"I'm going with you." His voice was flat and unwavering.

"By the Provider! I don't have time for this! Get outta my way." Cloi raised a fist as she spoke.

"Do you even know where you are going? Have you ever been past that door? Well, I have. I can get you through. Just take me with you."

"Fine, whatever, just don't expect me to wait for you if something goes wrong."

Rhom could feel the tension. He looked back to see if anyone had noticed, only to see the two Vigrop guards pointing at them.

"Cloi, we need to go now," Rhom said. The door was a good fifteen meters from where they were. Rhom ran, too scared to look back. Cloi and the unknown Crelli were right on his tail. They dashed toward the exit, several reptilian pursuers not far behind. Pushing through the door, the three of them slammed it shut and threw their entire weight against it.

"Find something big to block this door." Rhom looked around. There was a rolling cart filled with rock samples. He pushed it back to the door.

"Good," Cloi said as Rhom got closer. Quickly, he tipped the cart on its side, loudly spilling the contents against the metal door. "We have to keep moving!" she continued, pointing to another door on the far side of the room. The three of them dashed across the room and out into a long, narrow hall. The dimly lit corridor was lined with heavy metal doors. As they made their way past, Rhom noted each door was numbered, and a unique mark had been placed after the numbers on some doors.

"What is that symbol?" he asked.

"It is the mark of the Remplancant," the other Crelli said. "It would not be wise to open any door with that mark on it." His tone was heavy.

Rhom decided not to pry any further. He would ask Cloi later. They ran down the corridor toward where it ended in a "T," and Cloi turned to the left.

"Wait, not that way. Come, follow me. There is an armory down here," the unknown Crelli said.

Cloi looked down at the ragged clothes they were wearing.

"Lead on, uh...."

"Rota, the name is Rota. " He shifted his stance a bit as he spoke, as if to better present his strength, which was awkward since he was short and gawky.

"Ok then, Rota. Take us to the armory."

Taking the right turn at top speed, they ran down the hall.

R hom, Rota, and Cloi made their way to the armory with surprisingly little resistance. The few guards they saw were easily avoidable. Cloi tried the door to the armory. It was locked. Rota stepped up.

"I got this." He was grinning. A thin metal file was in his left hand, the other held a small needlefish bone.

"Well, by all means, hurry up," Cloi replied. After Rota fiddled with the lock for a few moments with no luck, she said, "Bah, this is taking too long. Rhom, take over and give it a try. I will be right back." She ran back down the hall they came from.

Rhom looked at Rota, shrugged his shoulders and said, "Well, I don't know anything about locks, but I will give it a try." He held his hand out to Rota for the tools. Rota extended his arm to hand over the tools and then stopped. His eyes widened and jaw dropped. His hand trembled. The tools slid slowly from his hand and clanged on the floor. Rhom was staring at him, confused, when he felt a heavy presence behind him.

"I-I wasn't really going to open it," Rota stammered "I was only doing as the master asked. He said watch for any trouble, he did. T-t-t-old me to bring them to him. I was just keeping my eyes on them."

Rhom felt the grip of two strong hands on both of his upper arms. A small group of Crelli surrounded him and Rota. The situation made no sense. First, why was Rota afraid of these Crelli? Second, why were Crelli freely walking around the Vigrop camp? Last, why did they look familiar?

The heavy sounds of a heated scuffle emanated from the hallway Cloi had just entered. Rhom tried to call out and was instantly silenced by a heavy hand. A few moments later, she emerged, hands bound behind, driven forward by her captors.

"Get your hands off me, Delpar! I can walk on my own," Cloi said.

"Delpar?" Rhom thought aloud. He looked again and, in a moment, it clicked. "Jambat!" Quickly, he scanned the room for Terth. He had so many questions. Nothing made sense. The Jambat team led the trio of fugitives to a large chamber with a domed roof. Rhom could see this was a training facility of some type. Examining the gear of these Jambat, he knew there was something different going on. The Visatae cylinders were larger than the standard issue. The cylinder also had slots along the sides, and he could see wings on their backs.

A door slid open to their left. Rhom felt a heavy wave pass through his head and a low roar filled his ears. Wincing in pain, he went slack in the grip of his captor. Cloi glanced his way slightly but resumed her stern focus on the new presence entering the room.

The rush of "interference" flooding Rhom was overwhelming. He could hear voices. It was like that time he heard Yereni screaming in his head, except this was many voices. Rhom used all his attention to slow the voices.

He closed his eyes and tried to focus on happy thoughts. First, because of the connected situation, he thought of Yereni, but the bad way they left each other was not a happy thought for him. Rhom went back into his mind, past his time with Uncle Brawzen and Terth. He thought back to his mother.

As he focused on memories of his childhood, one voice rose above the others—the static noise of many voices converged into one. It was the voice from the woods. The one he had hoped to meet again.

"What is this?" he asked.

"You have been alone for so long. I will be with you soon," was the reply.

"I am so confused; how can I get to you?" Rhom was intently focusing, trying to hear her.

"Follow the chosen ones. They will bring you to me."

Rhom did not understand. "How will I know who the chosen ones are?"

"They are with you now. Listen to them, feel their energy, embrace them all."

A hard blow jarred him from his state.

"Get up and face Skelkiz," Craznak said. Rhom looked up to find a Vigrop wearing a blue bone-like harness hovering above him, wings humming behind him.

"The Remplancant has given you favor. Your spark is deemed worthy young Stranded," Skelkiz proclaimed.

Rhom could hear his voice, but his thoughts were also being broadcast on a faster wavelength. Rhom knew what Skelkiz was going to say before he said it. A clarity of being overwhelmed Rhom. He could hear their thoughts all around him. It was painful to take it all in at once. He knew these Crelli. It was Terth's whole Jambat team: Moori, Sheidel, Delpar, Craznak, Valden, Berendi, all of them. Rhom looked around again, but no Terth.

Cloi could see the pain and struggle Rhom was going through. Try as she might, she was bound for the time being.

"Come here Rota, you fool!" Skelkiz commanded.

"Master, see, I found rebels in the camp. You asked me to keep an eye on the camp, and see I found them." Rota was cowering before the Vigrop leader.

"Silence. You have served your purpose. Now that your cover is exposed, I have no use for you." With that, Skelkiz waved his hand. Rhom could hear his thoughts and the response from Berendi.

"No!" Rhom screamed, but it was too late. Berendi lunged directly at Rota. In a blink, his monsu lanced Rota between the eyes. His body crumpled to the floor.

Skelkiz turned his head sharply to face Cloi. "You! You are not on my list."

Rhom knew what was going to happen next. A flood of emotions overwhelmed him. He was not going to lose her too. So much pain and turmoil over the past few months had driven dark spikes into his heart. Rhom felt a power rise in him.

"No more!" Rhom spoke under his breath. He tried to move in her direction. Two of the newly upgraded Jamtori shifted to intercept. The wings on their backs flared into position.

"NO MORE!" Rhom screamed. He could feel the thoughts across the room waver. Craznak's grip on Rhom's upper arms loosened.

Scrunching down, Rhom broke free. He continued to project his command to "Halt" while running toward Cloi, who also appeared dazed. Rhom pulled her away from the team and across the room. The voices were still there, but Rhom continued to press his thoughts louder, loud enough to drown the others from his mind. He cupped his hands under Cloi's armpits, hefted her up, and dragged her through the exit. He slammed the door shut and locked it. He was losing focus; the strain on his head was incredible.

Cloi looked up at him, eyes wide. The pounding of monsu could be heard on the other side of the door. It would not be long before the attackers broke through. He could already see large blisters appearing on the surface of the door from the impaling force.

"We need to move," Cloi said. Rhom nodded in agreement. He had lost any sense of language for the moment. The two escapees ran up the sloping tunnel. Pressing on, a notable freshness could be detected in the air. The change energized their weary muscles. Turning another corner, Cloi froze. Rhom bumped directly into her. He peered around her; it was an opening, a large natural cave entrance, and the sky beyond.

The area was bustling with activity. Vigrop were hosteling large carts of supplies, equipment, and prisoners to staging areas along several railways. This had to be the location where Yereni and he had been taken to after being captured at the outpost.

Rhom and Cloi crouched and then shuffled over to an enormous pile of ropes, netting, and other various-sized containers. Getting through the chaotic symphony of Vigrop activity would not be easy. Cloi turned to Rhom. "Do you think you can do it again?" He looked at her slightly, cocking his head in a confused way. "You know," she pumped her head up and down quickly. "The brain freeze thing." Rhom was at first kind of miffed, still feeling pressure along the back of his head. He looked at her and then turned to assembled Vigrop. He closed his eyes, trying to hone his focus on their thoughts. He could sense a low vibration of noise but nothing distinct. Rhom opened his eyes and turned to Cloi.

"It's no use. I don't know what I am trying to do," he said.

"C'mon, you are made of better than that. Remember who you are. You are Crelli from the Havens. You have taken all the tests for the Jambat even if you did not go to the selection like the others. I know you can do it. Try, just try. Find that spark deep down. I know you can do it. Just remember what is at stake here. If we cannot escape this place, there may be no Havens to return to."

Rhom felt a heavy cloak of dread fall upon him. "Is it that bad?" He could see familiar faces, friends, and people he had known his whole life before his eyes. He pictured their faces staring at him and, as if by a sudden wind, their faces blurred and were swept away. The reality of a world with no free Crelli terrified him. Rhom reached out one more time.

Once again, closing his eyes, he searched the cavern maw for voices. A shock of surprise shook him. Opening his eyes, he looked across the opening to the far side of the clearing. In a low, solemn voice, he exclaimed, "Terth, Terth is here."

As soon as Rhom had sensed Terth, a slight tinge of awareness alerted the young Jambat to Rhom's presence. Terth paused and turned his attention to the large room. Leaping up, he hovered in the center of the cavern, the wings from his back humming in rhythmic pulses. He scanned the room and darted directly for Rhom and Cloi.

"Rhom, you should come with me." Terth's tone was flat and emotionless.

Rhom looked at Terth.

"What are you doing here, Terth? Why are you serving the Vigrop? What has this Skelkiz done to you?" Rhom had so many pent-up emotions his voice quivered.

"Skelkiz has shown us the way to end the wars, a way for all to be at peace, a way for us to win. I will become the commander of a grand army, an army greater than any Jamtori in history. We will be the Dobai, and I will lead the way for the Crelli of the future. I won't let anyone get in my way. I know what you can do Rhom. The Visatae have shown me. You can help me succeed. We can do this together. Your ability can convince those who oppose you to submit. Come with me." Terth was still hovering above them. He held his hand down toward Rhom as he finished his last statement.

"We will not submit to you!" Cloi shouted. She had successfully separated one net from the pile, which she now threw at Terth. Rhom knew it was a fruitless attempt. He could read Terth's thoughts and the extra sensual inputs of the Visatae on Terth's back. His body quickly darted down, bringing him face-to-face with Cloi.

"I can see why Skelkiz wants you gone. You are indeed a nuisance."

"Run Rhom!" she shouted. Rhom jumped to his feet and sprinted for the open air. Terth turned to chase him. Cloi now freely darted to the left toward the closer wall and began her dash to escape.

Rhom was running full speed, his mind racing over another shocking reality. Was his mind truly fractured? Nothing, not a single memory, could be trusted. As he ran, he let out a howl. His wail rose as he ran.

Cloi could hear Rhom screaming in her head. Vigrop all over the staging area stopped their activity. The sound was intense. Cloi felt it pass through her like a hot wind. She was nearing the entrance, just a few more steps to the open world.

Rhom had run haphazardly. Perhaps he thought this would help him evade Terth, but the zigzag course had taken longer for him to reach the opening than Cloi.

Rhom's voice was still raised in a now overwhelming chord of sorrow. The sound forced those within range to cower in pain. Covering their ears to dull the sound was useless; the pain could not be audibly quelled. It burned inside of all of them. Tears ran down his face. When Rhom was close enough, Cloi extended her hand to him. Clasping him by the arm together they rappelled violently down the hillside.

Terth paused at the opening. He watched as the two leaped over a low rock wall and tumbled into the brush and disappeared, then gave a small, twisted smile. Turning to reenter the cavern, he quickly flew down and punched the first Vigrop within reach directly across the jaw, dropping the poor unsuspecting worker to the ground.

Rhom awoke with a start, only to quickly lie down again. His head was throbbing. He leaned to his side to see he was lying on a platform high in the trees. Cloi was hunched next to a large branch, looking out over the canopy of leaves, her silhouette visible in the night light.

"We need to move now. It may not be the smartest way to travel, but it is better that we go at night to avoid being seen."

She slid over toward Rhom and continued. "I want you to come with me to the North—to a safe place away from the Jamtori, and the Visatae. To a place where you can recover."

Rhom looked toward the east. A faint glow could be seen in the distance. They were about two day's journey from the Havens, from home. He wondered what Uncle Brawzen was doing. Rhom could recall the days of running around the trees, in and out of the thickets and up into the highest branches. Chasing Terth who somehow always ended up with the item Rhom wanted or needed.

He needed something to take his mind off that

last encounter with Terth. Suddenly Rhom blurted out. "Yereni!"

"Who?"

"Yereni—she is still there. I didn't even get a chance to fix it. We must save her. I have to say sorry. C'mon, we need to go back now!" Rhom was intent.

"Rhom, there are many Crelli there who need to be saved. We cannot possibly go back now. There are only two of us. I still don't even know how we escaped. The only way is to go north. The Separatists reject the Visatae and live as free Crelli. They will help us. There are hunters. and many who were Keepers before joining the Separatists."

"But, Yereni could be in trouble. She helped me when I was hurt. She is my friend. They killed her mother, and I couldn't even help." Rhom was losing it again, more stupid emotions rising to the top.

"How are you going to help now, then?" Cloi said. "You need to have a plan. The Separatists can help. I will help. I promise when the time comes, I will be right there with you. We will find Yereni, and everything will be ok. Now can we move on? The sooner we head north, the sooner we can create a plan."

"When we come back, we set all the Crelli free, including Terth and the other Jambat. Agreed?" Rhom looked directly into Cloi's face. She could see the spark of hope glinting in his eyes.

"All of them" she replied.

"Ok, Cloi take me North." His response was flat and empty.

Cloi studied him momentarily before responding.

"Well, ok scruffytuff. Let's get moving. I am hungry and know you must be too. Let's see what we can find that way." Cloi pointed across the platform toward an opening in the foliage. Rhom half smiled as she messed with his hair. Cloi had been kind to him when he was small and though she could be tough when the situation called for it, her fair nature created a great balance.

"Anything you say. Just get us far from here, please." Rhom was ready to go.

That night, the two covered a fair portion of ground, creating a safer distance from the cavern. Rhom was able to climb a tall tree just before daybreak. Peering back over the green roof of leaves, he could see the waterfalls that fed the great lake near the Havens to his right. The cave must have been east of them in Bellop territory. They had crossed the forest between the lake and his old home in the night. A Vigrop camp with Crelli Jambat guards in Bellop territory was indeed unheard of. Whatever Terth was engaged in, if not stopped, was going to change their world forever. Rhom hoped it was not too late.

The next few nights were uneventful. They scurried through the upper branches of the forest, occasionally encountering a beast or two. Just before sunset, Cloi would quietly nudge Rhom from his halfway sleep. Sleeping wedged between the forks of the branches left a lot of kinks and sore spots.

Cloi was a cautious guide and an experienced hunter. No doubt Rhom would have been dead many times over if not for her presence. The feelings of uselessness, inadequacy, and guilt slowly crept in. To fight these feelings, Rhom would spend time thinking about the faces of those he cared about, primarily Terth, Uncle Brawzen, and Yereni. Every time it came to Yereni, Rhom would think about the voices. The one who called herself "Mother" was definitely not his mother. The more he thought about it, the crazier it all seemed. It was a vicious circle of questions and feelings that often made him nauseous. Once, when Cloi and Rhom had found a shady spot to sleep for the day, he tried talking to Cloi about the voices and the weird events that had occurred while near the new species of Visatae. Cloi was quick to tell him to wait until they got to the camp. There would be help for him there. Rhom did not bring it up again.

Rhom could now tell from the direction they were headed the valley was behind them and the two of them were ascending the mountain range bordering the northwest. The nights were colder, and the broad trees thinned, making way for a prickly thin branched tree resembling large tumbleweeds. Rhom had never been so far from home. The new region touched all his senses. He found the experience calming. It was enough of a distraction to ease his mind to some degree.

Once they reached the edge of the forest, Cloi said there was no point in moving at night. With the colder nights, it made sense to hunker up back-to-back for warmth at the base of a low ridge or boulder. Rhom noted that the number of other creatures had dwindled. Food was scarce. Cloi showed him how to dig up the roots of a short, waxy leafed plant. The root ball contained a crispy watery flesh that was sweet.

They had traveled most of this morning on the ground between the large thorn trees toward a tall, sheer formation of rock. Rhom was looking back over the valley, amazed at how long it went on and wondering where the Havens was in the middle of the thickness. Even the lake was gone from sight.

Suddenly Cloi spoke, "There, do you see the smoke?"

She pointed further up the hill to a tall cliff face that seemed to run forever in either direction, blocking their ascending path. Rhom squinted as he turned to gaze up ahead. He could indeed see wispy smoke curling over and around the rock formations ahead.

"I see it! " he exclaimed.

Just as he spoke, a pair of Crelli sprang out of nowhere and blocked the path.

"State your business or return the way you came and make it quick. We don't have time for any worm-lovers." The sentry extended his arm as he spoke. In his hand was a pole about half his height. As he finished his last words, the pole extended in either way with a slinging sound like a monsu. The lower spike pierced the rocky ground with a spark.

Cloi stiffened into a tall straight pose, both arms down flat to her side. "Advanced Recon Scout Cloi, returning with information vital to all of us." She stared into the sentry's eyes. The two looked at Rhom and then back to Cloi.

The first sentry turned to the other. "Go and get the captain. I will keep these two here."

Cloi spoke. "Sit, Rhom, this may take a little time."

Rhom sat down on a rock nearby and observed the sentry. He looked like any other Crelli back home. The difference was in the gear. First, he noticed the thick vest under the harness and a hooded cloak which was folded in half and pinned up from one shoulder to the other in a short swag. The monsu staff Rhom had already noted when it sparked. The other thing Rhom noted was the thick boots. Boots were something new. Rhom thought about it, his own cold feet which were recently sore from trudging the rocky ground, and realized what a benefit this item could be.

They waited an eternity, which in reality was about thirty minutes. The sun was just beyond its zenith for the day and the rock ledges beyond cast shadows whose tips crept slowly toward the group. Cloi stood. Rhom could see the second sentry and another Crelli walking toward them.

"Well, I'll be a bearded sloazian tree walker! Cloi, I never expected to see you again. I heard they had captured you," the captain spoke.

"Hello, Worlz," she replied.

Rhom noticed she reacted to the captain a little bashfully. Not at all the confident, bossy, sharp-tongued Crelli she was around the Havens. Rhom smiled slightly, having discovered her secret. He couldn't wait to bring this up next time they were alone and confirm the theory.

"I need to see Berhpas right away" she continued.

"By all means, head up there. I trust you still remember the way?" Captain Worlz sniggered playfully.

"I just got here, don't start with those navigation jokes." She gave him a small dagger glare. The captain roared.

"So glad to have you back, Cloi the Wanderer," he responded and laughed again.

"C'mon Rhom, my feet are cold, and I am hungry. The sooner we get up there, the sooner we can rest." Cloi's response was snippy. Rhom figured she was embarrassed for being called a wanderer, and he quietly followed her.

Just before heading up the slope, he turned to face the valley. "Soon," he thought, "I will be back soon, Yereni. Terth. I promise I will be back with an army of Crelli, and we will rescue you both."

Skelkiz opened the door to the cell. Yereni's back faced the door. The food left for her remained untouched.

Skelkiz was in full nasty mode today and his tone showed it. "I will give you one more chance to tell me how you maimed an entire unit of Vigrop. Even the Bellop brute with them was afraid to come back."

Yereni did not respond. She remained motionless.

"Sssssince, you continue to refussse my requessstsssss, I thought sssomething more drassstic might be in order." He continued, "If you will not talk to me, perhapssss, you will talk to him."

Two Vigrop guards led a bound figure into the room. Skelkiz turned from the girl toward the new guest.

"I don't think I need to do any introductions." He looked back at Yereni. "Ssssay hello to daddy."

"Yereni, don't say anything to him!" Bendohl shouted.

Her ears twitched, and she turned her head. One eye was swollen shut and a thin cut spanned her left cheek from mouth to ear. Her eyes glared at Skelkiz.

"There she issss." He waved at her with his long index finger. "If you refuse to talk, I will slowly remove pieces from his body until you do." Skelkiz rubbed his reptilian hands together. "I give you until the morning to figure it out."

The door closed and Yereni slid from the bed to her father. Tears rolled down her face as she hugged him with her arms wrapped firmly around his head.

"I...I...went looking for you," Bendohl said with a quiver. "I found a burnt outpost. Your mother's charm was in the remains. I looked everywhere for you."

Yereni continued to weep. The lid was off the box and her heart poured out. "She's gone, Mumma's gone." Yereni squeezed the words out between gasps for breath from the crying. Bendohl, one good leg, twitched, and he shrugged his shoulders, the bonds across his midsection uncomfortable. Yereni looked down. Her eyes were afraid to meet his.

"They killed her, those terrible Vigrop. Then something happened. I don't know what it was, but it came from me, Poppa. I hated them all and then it happened." She lost it again, more sobbing than words.

"Yereni, it is ok—I can fix it. Just get me loose and we can talk about this together. I promise you, once we talk this through, I can make it all better." Bendohl nudged her shoulder with his head with affection. Yereni moved her hands down and methodically removed the cords binding her father. Finally free, Bendohl motioned for help to stand.

"Without my apparatus, I am worthless." He looked older to Yereni. Bendohl continued, "Help me over to the bed so we can talk." Yereni was spent. She didn't want to talk. The re-opened wound from losing her mother was ugly and infectious.

"You need to rest, Poppa." She responded, hoping to dodge the painful conversation she knew must happen.

"You heard that awful Skelkiz. If we don't come up with the answers he wants, we are BOTH as good as dead. Now tell me what happened. Why did you leave with your mother? Where was she taking you? Did she say anything about me?" Bendohl looked directly at Yereni.

"It wasn't like that at all. I was with Rhom; we were eating some fish. Mother followed me there."

"Who is Rhom?"

"He is a boy from the Havens. I found him in the woods. He was injured, and I helped him. I should have left him to die, then mama would still be alive."

"The Havens? What have I always said about Crelli?" He was stern. "Especially from the Havens. They polluted the Citadel with politics. If my plan had been used all Crelli would be empowered. Instead, we have the Jamtori, the Jaruvian Order, and that idiot Masari of theirs." Bendohl paused. "Go on, my dear, please continue."

"Rhom and I were at the outpost. Mama followed us and was scolding me for taking food to him. We were attacked by a group of Vigrop slave hunters. We fought— mama, and me—we fought hard. Then a Bellop showed up. He was huge and grabbed Mama." She knew this point was going to come. Yereni tried to be tough and choke back the tears. "He killed her; the Bellop killed her." Yereni let out a tremendous wail and cried some more.

Bendohl let her cry it out.

"What happened after? I heard that Skelkiz say the Vigrop were burned."

"I don't know. I was angry and something happened. I could see the room and my hands. Everything was alive, tingly. I felt something passing through me. I felt connected to the ground, the trees, the animals, to everything. I felt strong. I was going to make them pay." As she spoke, she straightened up.

"How did it stop?" Bendohl asked.

"Rhom—was the one who stopped me. I wanted to avenge Mama, and he stopped me. I heard him in my head. He had no business in my head. It was his fault she died. I hate him." She punched the wall.

"Do you think you can do it again?" Bendohl asked. "If we work together, maybe you can do it again. You can get even with that boy." Yereni looked at her father for a moment. His mouth opened to ask something, then paused. A moment of silence passed as she thought back to that painful event. It was truly not her fault, it was Rhom's.

"I will try," she said.

"I think if I tell the Vigrop what I used to do before my accident, about my inventions, I may buy us some time together. I will ask them when they return. Perhaps together in time, we can find out the source of this power and use it to help us get free."

Yereni nodded and slumped down on the bed. Her already sore body was now overfatigued from the expelling of pent-up pain. Turning to her side, she curled up and closed her eyes. No more talking for now. Bendohl looked over at her. He took a deep breath and closed his eyes, letting his chin nod on his chest; a broad smile was on his face.

"Where is he? Where is that mangy kallopod farmer?"

Rhom looked up from the table to see a grinning Uncle Brawzen swim through the sea of patrons toward him, only to be scooped up in a giant squeeze. "I am so glad you are safe, my boy," he said, placing Rhom back down and holding him squarely by the shoulders.

Rhom was dumbfounded; he rubbed the back of his head and pivoted his heel in the new pair of boots he was wearing.

"I'm sorry I ran out, Uncle." Rhom said.

"We all have decisions we look back on. The question is what you are going to do to move forward." Brawzen ran his hand over Rhom's head and messed his hair a little. "Now, tell me how you got here." He looked over at Cloi and winked. "Did you get lost or something?" Cloi rolled her eyes and huffed into her drink. Liquid splashed from the cup and onto her face. She let out a quick "ohhoo" and grabbed a cloth from the table next to her.

"Terth—something has gone wrong. He, well, he

has joined with the Vigrop. Him and some of the other new Jambats." Rhom was clearly shaken.

"Did they have wings?" Uncle Brawzen asked.

"This is something that needs to be discussed in council," Cloi said, eyeing the room. Brawzen cautiously looked around. He adjusted his position and turned again to Rhom.

"Tell me about this scar on your leg. It looks like it was painful."

Rhom told Uncle Brawzen all about the cornas and the radoacs and showed him the scars. Brawzen sat and listened, not saying a word. Suddenly Rhom stopped.

"Wait a minute, why are YOU here? How do you even know about this place?" Rhom gave Uncle Brawzen the most determined look as he asked.

"When the lab exploded..." Brawzen started over, "Actually, before the tragedy that affected so many in the Havens, I was a Keeper, you know. From the first discovery of the Visatae, some had a dislike for the communion. The Jaruvian Order had us tracking some of the more, uh, outspoken dissenters." You could tell this was important, as many in the room had stopped their conversations and turned to hear what he was going to say.

Brawzen resumed, "Well, a few of us Keepers didn't like the way the Jamtori hid things from the public. We'd heard rumors of Vigrop sneaking into the Citadel under cover and, of course, the growing political power exercised by the Masari and his acolytes. The opposition was led chiefly by Berhpas. He spoke out openly against the creation of the Lab. He believed Crelli should develop their strength and not rely on the Vigrop or the Visatae. Berhpas saw the Visatae as a corruption of our faith in Jaru."

"But what did you believe?" Rhom asked.

117

"Me, I was torn. You see, my sister, Vaetris, Terth's mother, was part of the lab. She worked closely with your parents and others. They were a tight crew: Sherundi your mother, Thaan your father, Vaetris, Teleg, Ahkaiyee, and Bendohl. That group was the driving force behind all the rapid progress in the Havens. The vespridium mines, the testing machines, the Rookery, the advanced motors for the monsu and tonsu, and many other things." Brawzen took a sip of the drink which was placed before him. The room was silent, waiting for him to continue.

Returning the cup to the board, he wiped his face with the back of his hand and continued. "So yes, I was conflicted. I did not want to spy on our own, but I could see the advantages we were gaining from the innovation at the Labs."

"The explosion changed everything. The Masari blamed Berhpas for the incident, claiming any who had opposed the Citadel as traitors to Jaru and enemies of the Havens. Those who could flee came here to the mountains. A network of signs marked along particular trees led the way. Many misleading and false marks were placed among the trees as well. If you forget the marks, you could end up wandering the forest for days." Rhom looked over at Cloi. He smiled. The mystery of "Cloi the Wanderer" had been solved.

"But what about those who didn't escape?" Rhom asked.

Cloi sat up and looked at Brawzen. He nodded his head, and she spoke. "That was my mission, to find the missing Crelli. When I first arrived a cycle ago, it was by accident. I remember being rescued from the explosion. I never understood why I did not agree with the Jamtori. Recently, Berhpas showed me something, an item that confirmed my suspicions of the Jamtori. I vowed I would find the missing ones, which led me to the mines and you, Rhom."

"It was the same for me, Rhom," Brawzen said. "It wasn't until recently that I found my way here. Although when the responsibility to care for you and Terth fell on me those many years ago, I considered leaving the Havens to remove the two of you from the eyes of the Masari. Perhaps things would be different now."

Rhom lifted his head and looked directly at Uncle Brawzen. "You have done your best. There is not a time I can recall when you did not try. I am thankful I had the freedom to learn, even when I knew I could not join the Jamtori—something I am glad never happened now."

"Never mind that. Now let me finish." Brawzen continued. "After you left, I waited several days hoping you would come back. Worry got the best of me, and I left to see if I could find you. I left a message with Widow Splincer in case you came back. I checked in the normal places you and Terth would visit and nothing." Brawzen stopped for a moment to scratch his ear.

"My search grew wider as I circled away from the Havens, sweeping the forest for any sign of you, fearing the worst. I came across a terrible scene at an outpost where I found the body of a female Crelli who had been mauled by something. It was there that I ran into someone from the past. It was a survivor from the lab."

"It was his mate who had died at the outpost, and he was looking for his daughter, a girl about your age. Her name was Yereni." Rhom felt slightly sick at the dreaded truth. Yereni was now like him, cursed by the Lab, cursed to lose family. That stupid event tainted everything close to him.

As Brawzen said the name Yereni, Cloi turned with a snap and stared directly at Rhom.

Brawzen continued his story, "Bendohl shot me with a drugged dart. He must have thought it would kill me or he wouldn't have told me his plans. Bendohl wants to take over the Jamtori. He has found a way, an evolved Visatae, and wants to use them to conquer the entire realm. He thinks peace can only be achieved if he becomes the Sursamain of all Crellantan ruling over us, the Vigrop, and even the Bellop."

"Terth is currently beyond my reach. Growing up, his desire was to be the best and prove he was not weak, but what he does not know is he is fighting himself more than anything else. You are different. I would often see you let Terth win, even when you were the better of the two. You would rather choose peace at the cost of being thought of as less. This is what I was trying to say so many days ago."

Brawzen investigated his empty cup, stood up from the table, placing both hands firmly down in front of him. He looked sternly into Rhom's face and spoke his ending lines for the night. "Tomorrow you will meet Berhpas. He will continue to explain the truth about your family. Once he has told you the rest, you will have to decide. Are you going to be the warbringer or the peacemaker?"

Rhom spent the night restlessly tossing between dreams and staring at the ceiling. Dawn's rays spread across the horizon. The sound of morning preparations reached his ears. His dreams had been filled with a gregarious mix of emotions, memories, and fantasy. The sum of it was, today he was going to learn more about his parents. With the confusing visions of his mother that had occurred over the past few months, Rhom hoped to find clarity after speaking with Berhpas.

Emerging from one of the rounded domes scattered across the clearing, Rhom walked to the center of the encampment to warm himself by one of the cooking fires. His hands were cold and clammy from nerves. An energetic quiver of anticipation flushed through him from head to foot. The Crelli, busy with their morning tasks, fluttered in and out of the clearing. Many would give him a silent affirmative nod as they whirled about. After a short while, Rhom felt a forceful presence behind him. He felt a firm hand rest on his shoulder.

Rhom turned to see Captain Worlz standing there. "Follow me," the captain said.

The two stitched a path amongst the huts and various other resource buildings to the foot of the cliff face deep in the clearing. A small pool lay before them and beyond a single tree spread its gnarled arms. Rhom realized it was like the tumble trees from just below the Separatist camp. The difference between this tree and the tumble trees was the green spiny leaves covering the outer edge. The hollow in the center reminded Rhom of the childhood hangout he shared with Terth back near the Havens. The entire scene felt both foreign and familiar.

Rhom heard a strong deep voice from behind speak, "You may leave us, Worlz."

Turning with a smooth twist. Captain Worlz saluted in the most efficiently correct way Rhom had ever seen. The presentation surpassed any performed at the Citadel in years. Berhpas nodded and Captain Worlz made his way back to the communal area near the front wall.

"Now, shall we see just who you are and what pieces Jaru provided you, hmm?" His voice was low and smooth, like slow water over rock. The mention of Jaru gave Rhom a slight sting. With so many truths and undone truths, a belief in Jaru was off-putting and left a sour taste to Rhom. Berhpas noticed and responded.

"I see you have been updated on some things. In time, you will come to understand much more than you may care to know. But for now, let us sit and enjoy this morning before it escapes."

Rhom looked down to see they had moved to the far side of the pool and were at the opening of the woven tree. They must have traveled from the far side while Berhpas was speaking, but Rhom did not remember walking.

The two entered the confines of the branched chamber. In the center, upon a round stone, a small tray of fruit and a decanter with two cups were assembled.

Rhom sat down and looked directly at Berhpas. The other was already seated with his eyes closed. Rhom could see his eyes shift slightly behind the lids.

The pause gave Rhom time to review Berhpas and the surroundings. Berhpas was stout, and his hair was long for a Crelli; most choose to keep their hair short to avoid becoming trapped or entangled by the trees they traveled through. His hands were clean and his clothes as well. He wore a tunic of natural fiber with light symbols stained along the hem, which reminded Rhom of the testing wall back at home.

Jambat candidates would often leave the regular daily lessons to spend time with the Masari. Rhom would sneak peeks during regular school sessions. From what Rhom could determine, the testing wall was designed to teach you how to relax your mind and allow the Masari to determine your compatibility with a Visatae host. The symbols would glow blue and then dim as students took turns inside the small dome at the base.

An instant spark of an idea came to Rhom. The covering over the island was designed with the symbols on purpose. This was an outdoor testing dome. The openings shifted into familiar shapes remarkably similar to the wall back home and a faint glow emitted from the edges. A smile crossed the face of Berhpas. Then, with his eyes still closed, he spoke.

"So, you have been given something, after all. We can work with this. Yes, I can see now why Brawzen was torn between the two. We must explore this, but first, we must eat." Berhpas waved his hand before the table, indicating for Rhom to select something from the plate. Grabbing a handful of plinth nuts and a larger piece of fruit, he returned to his place. Berhpas finished a small, round fruit before speaking.

"I knew your parents." Rhom stopped chewing and looked up. Berhpas continued, "I was part of the Jaruvian Order before the Visatae were revealed. As one of the stewards to the previous Masari, I worked as an intermediary with the Jamtori. Your father and a group of youth came to the Citadel with their discovery: vespridium. The material is not evil itself, but the possession of it has divided our society."

"Your parents were not bad people; they were only caught up in events that were beyond their control. I know some of this Brawzen has shared with you. What you may not know is that you and several others were the results of a carefully conceived plan to use the vespridium to unlock the unknown potential of the Crelli."

Berhpas took a drink and brushed the lap of his tunic before returning to his story. "Bendohl, a researcher at the lab in the Proving Grounds, believed the abilities gained by merging with the Visatae were latent within all Crelli, and the Visatae were simply tapping into it. He sought to move the Crelli beyond that dependency. More than a few volunteer couples were selected to provide their unborn Crelli as test subjects."

Rhom felt lightheaded. With all the events that had happened to him recently, his general conception of Crellentanian history and beliefs had lost most of its hold on him. He felt the next sentence would sever any sense of obligation to honor his parents' memory by leading an exemplary life. His actions growing up were shadowed, always shadowed by the vision of his mother judging his every move. He weighed his decisions against the imagined concept of his mother's grace.

"You were one of those subjects. Originally there were twenty-one; several did not even make it through the first stages of development. Fifteen were born over an eight-season cycle. Some of those were born with abnormalities no Crelli should have ever witnessed. In the end, seven of you were selected to be the next level of Crelli. I know this from the reports sent to the Masari." Berhpas looked upon Rhom. The watery, glazed eyes revealed the depth of truth's arrow.

"So, even the Masari was in on this? Justice must be given to those families. The Crellan must be told." Rhom clenched his fist as he spoke.

"In time, first you must hear the entire account. Once I have finished, you will know what must be done. Now, as I said, there were seven of you before the explosion. Terth and you, we know. Brawzen had some influence with the Keepers and was able to retain the two of you with the promise he would report any unusual occurrence to the Jamtori."

Rhom thought back to their childhood. He did often wonder how the two of them managed to escape reprimand from the monks during lessons. Perhaps they had been instructed to be lenient with them and they were not as clever as they imagined.

"Brawzen confirmed Bendohl's ward was or is still alive. I think you know this."

"Yereni," Rhom said under his breath just as Berhpas spoke her name.

"Yes, you know who she is, don't you? The question is, how well do you know her? Being raised by the mastermind himself, she may not be as she seems." Berhpas sipped a little from his drink. His eyelids were lowered making it difficult for Rhom to read.

"It is time we sharpened the tools you have been given. Rhom, we are going to explore the effect vespridium has had on you.

It was morning and Rhom was tired. Berhpas, with the help of Captain Worlz, went through various scenarios attempting to discover his latent abilities. They determined his strand was primarily psionic in origin, a combination of extrasensory perception, telepathy, and psychokinesis. During these exercises, Rhom learned that Worlz was also one of the Vespridium children.

He was older than Rhom by two seasons and was one of the first to survive the stranding process at the lab. Worlz was connected to all life in the forest. He described it as a general sense of empathy for what was around him. If the forest was in danger, he knew it long before others could sense it. The creatures in the forest revealed all.

It was unclear how far he could detect these shifts in energy, but it gave him enough time to be alert. Among the Crelli, he could sense the overall tone of the community. If he was out on patrol, it was difficult to isolate his team from the overwhelming background tension created by the presence of his team in the forest. Berhpas was teaching the captain how to project his influence on the emotions of the Crelli around him and in time on all life forms.

For Rhom, the calm demeanor of Berhpas combined with knowing that the captain was also a Strand eased his mind. Occasionally he would become frustrated with the questions and constant mental focus required, but Captain Worlz was there to provide support. At night Rhom would lie thinking about Yereni and Terth and the struggles they might go through with their strand emerging.

Berhpas cleared his throat and began "You have experienced enough instances to know when you are under the influence of your, shall we say, "gifts." Today we start to hone those skills. Cloi mentioned a game you may have played at home in the Havens. Perhaps you remember Flinter's Folly?"

Of course, Rhom remembered it. It was a game Terth was best at, and one Rhom was good at pretending to like. He wondered what this had to do with Strands.

"I remember it, but how will this help me right now?" The thought of Flinter's Folly reminded him of Yereni and the fun days at the empty outpost. It made him anxious thinking of her and the other Crelli stuck in those mines. More than anything, he wanted to get back and fix things with her. His mind wandered. Snap. Berhpas flicked a short wispy branch across Rhom's shoulder. It was enough to get his attention.

"Focus. Calm your mind. Find a place within your mind where you can feel confident, alert, and strong. It can be a memory, a dream. Any location physical or imagined as long as it is vivid."

Rhom closed his eyes. Images jumbled together raced by, zooming in and out of focus. The shapes reminded him of the symbols along the hem of Berhpas' robe. He tried to catch them as they passed. The shapes slowed, revealing a woven dome similar to the tumbletree sphere they were in and oddly like the hide-out back home. His mind was relaxed. A soft pulsing light could be seen coming from the edge of the surrounding lattice.

"Good. Now I want you to reach out with your senses. Find the flinter's around you. Imagine your thoughts as an extension of your physical body. If you let them detect you, it is over just like flinching in the game. Now bring yourself in. Nothing is beyond your mind."

Rhom, sweat forming along his brow, tried his best to see beyond his mind fort without leaving it. He could hear the water near them. He tuned it out. Next, the breeze across the leaves, he removed the sound. One by one, he cancelled the surrounding noises. Rhom could hear the thump of his heartbeat grow louder as he removed the other noises from his awareness. He pressed in, imagining he was climbing into his own body from the outside. Rhom looked into a dark pool. The rhythmic beat of his heart spread ripples across the top.

Rhom felt drawn to the water. He leaned forward, crouching low on all fours. The ripples slowed slightly. Going further, Rhom submerged his head below the surface. Silence met him. The peace was immense. He slid his whole body into the water and swam down. Just as he was getting used to the calm silence, a tingle of energy rolled down his spine. Rhom froze in the water. A distant shape could just be seen in the dim light of the pool. He cautiously swam toward it. Rhom could hear far-off noises. He realized it was another Crelli. Who? He could not determine. He wanted to get a closer look. Swimming behind the stranger, Rhom extended his hand to touch the other on the shoulder.

Suddenly, a curtain of light cut him off from the other figure. Rhom reeled back. At the same time, he realized his physical body. Am I breathing? Is my heart beating? How do I get back? He panicked. He felt like he was choking. Everything swirled around him. Rhom opened his eyes. He was gasping for air. His body was covered in sweat, his heart was racing. Flailing his arms about wildly grabbing at nothing, he finally felt the firm hand of the captain on his shoulder. A flood of calm commands brought him back to reality.

Once the chest-bursting pain, coughing, and sputtering ended, he spoke. "What was that light?" Rhom was both excited and scared.

"You got caught," Berhpas replied. "Our captain over here revealed his presence to your mind. He led you in and wham, closed the connection."

"I am sorry. Rhom, it was not meant to frighten you. I have trained with Berhpas for so long seeking resontas, I forget what it must feel like to someone new."

"Resontas?" Rhom was still reeling from the experience.

"It is an old Jaruvian mental exercise seeking a vacuous gap of consciousness. A simpler term would be 'empty mind.' You lose yourself to find yourself." Worlz seemed excited to share. Berhpas only nodded in agreement.

"I continue to seek complete resontas. It seems the vespridium stranded can achieve a higher-level awareness than those of the High Order of Jaru. The Masari claims he has found resontas, although I think he is exaggerating." Berhpas revealed a light-hearted slight smirk.

"How is it that the path inward seemed so easy?" Rhom asked.

"The platform we are on and the structure of the wood around us have been infused with vespridium. It is the same with the testing wall the Jamtori use when training younglings. The chamber where the hatching occurs in the Citadel is also infused." Berhpas replied.

"How do you know this?"

"I know because I am the one who infused it," Berhpas said. "In time, I will tell you more."

Rhom spent every spare hour in constant pursuit of honing his skills. Often, he would sleep on the little island in the training area. He spoke only with Berhpas and Worlz, who came by as duties allowed. It had been less than a month and the burden of saving Yereni persisted. He knew he was supposed to be focusing on the greater goal of freeing all the Crelli from the slavers, but he desperately wanted to return to her. To see her smile and simply enjoy an aimless day like they did in the past.

His ability to mind dive grew with each day. He had discovered he could mentally travel beyond the encampment by locating the guards who left the compound to patrol below the wall. If he could see them in the "silent pool" before they got too far away, Rhom could anchor his conscious to theirs undetected. Although Rhom could hear the thoughts of others as they went about their day, he could not penetrate their memories. If he concentrated, he could listen to a conversation between a few people. The odd thing about it was he did not know what they were speaking. Only what they were thinking, which in a way was both comical and frightfully truthful.

Worlz could still detect Rhom seven out of ten times during their practice sessions, but Rhom had dramatically improved. His desire to return to the mines pushed him beyond his limits. He became anxious and combative with Berhpas about his training. Rhom felt every day was one day too late to return.

Finally, one-day Berhpas did not appear at the waterside hut. Rhom sensed something was off-kilter and headed down the slope to the encampment. He could feel the tension increase as he closed the distance to the cantina. A crowd was gathered around a very battered and frail Crelli. Uncle Brawzen was propping the poor wretched soul's head as Cloi poured a warm broth into his mouth.

"They are killing us... Crelli. Our own Jamtori have betrayed us." The starving Crelli could barely get his words out.

Of course, Rhom knew this. He had seen it for himself. Part of him said, "Of course, that is why we need to get back. Only cowards hide from helping someone." The other part was guilt for staying here so long, safe, while others suffered far away.

The escapee turned to Rhom. "I was at the bellows the day you escaped, the mess you made, they tortured us, that leader Terth, he maimed many of us, he even killed his own people. He killed Crelli." The crowd turned and looked at Rhom with glinting eyes. It was true rumors had spread about Rhom and just what he was doing here. He had only arrived a month ago and the way he spent time with Berhpas, as if he were something special, had created some ill feelings in the community. The suffering Crelli's comments fanned the flame of jealousy within the crowd. It was as if they were looking for a reason to find him guilty of something, anything, and now they had it.

A few of the crowd shifted toward Rhom. He could tell by their posture that the intention was less than cordial. He tried a partial mind dive to locate their thoughts. He sensed a pulsing wall of negative thoughts. It wasn't harm he read, but fear.

They were afraid of him. What if he was there to harm them, like Terth?

Rhom spoke out, "Fellow Crellan, I know what he has felt. If it wasn't for Cloi and her bravery, I would still be there, too." The crowd eased slightly.

Cloi stood and picked up the conversation. "Rhom is not to blame here. It is true I have lingered here too long as well and others have been harmed from it. Seeing this brave Crellan, I am reminded of my own mistake. We need to go back and free the others. The time has come to rescue the captives and unite our people. Are there any brave Crelli among us? Rise up. End the suffering. It was I who brought Rhom here against his better judgment. He wanted to return and free others the night we escaped. I was the one who told him to wait. Well, wait we have. Rhom has suffered in silence while the one he cares about is imprisoned by those traitors and their savage Vigrop lackeys. Now is the time to be strong. What say you? Will you choose this day to free the forsaken Crellan or continue to hide in the rocks and dream of days past?"

The crowd was stone silent. A woman huddled against the outer wall of the cantina quietly sobbed. A young girl next to her consoled the shaken woman. A few of the bystanders studied the dirt around their feet, too ashamed to speak up.

"I will go." A voice spoke from behind Rhom. It was Worlz. "Even if none follow, I will go."

Uncle Brawzen stood. "As will I, I must see Terth with my own eyes. I must know if he has truly become a dreaded terror."

A few others spoke. A small band of supporters soon swelled into a mass of volunteers. Captain Worlz quickly assigned a group of his trained scouts the arduous task of gathering names and assessing the volunteer's potential capabilities. By the afternoon, the serious work of preparing to raid the mines and free the captives was in motion.

Rhom was not required to be present for any of the pre-planning since Cloi had been a captive too. Instead, he made his way up the hill toward the dais on the island. Berhpas was not to be found. Rhom made his way around the water to the base of the giant cliff toward the cave Berhpas occupied. Oddly, he realized only Berhpas entered or emerged. The thought of looking in had not occurred to Rhom until this moment.

As he drew close, an icy wave coursed through his chest. His arms became heavy and the hair along his nape stood tall, tight, and rigid. Passing through the low opening, Rhom walked down a short tunnel. Each step became incrementally heavier.

"Hello? Berhpas, are you there?" Rhom's words were swallowed by the darkness. Exiting the tunnel, he found the cave opened into a round room filled with multiple openings leading to passages of unknown length. An assembly of blankets and pillows was piled in one corner, appearing to have been recently used. Directly across from the pile of bedding on a large flat wall, a mandala-style design of interwoven symbols had been etched into the stone.

Rhom approached the wall. Extending his hand, he traced one of the symbols with his finger. A soft glow trailed along the surface behind his finger. The wall was infused with vespridium. Rhom centered himself in front of the inscription. Pressing his open hands against the wall, he instituted a mind-dive. Instead of the dark, silent pool, Rhom was transported to the compound outside. Immediately, he knew something was different. He was above the ground a good fifteen feet. The world was alive with vibrant colors, much different from the dark shadows of the mind pool. The effect was a complete contrast to Berhpas' definition of resontas. Rhom found with some slight effort he could shift his momentum to "will" his way in any direction. He urged his way to the edge of the camp. The overlapping thoughts of the Crelli below chimed in his ears. He could isolate an individual thought path if he desired.

Searching the camp, Rhom located Worlz outside the entrance to one of the storehouses. The captain tilted his head slightly and scanned the area. He had been in conversation with one of the recently promoted scouts. Worlz quickly dismissed his subordinate. Turning and walking away from the storehouse, he sat down, back against a large rock which obscured him from any passer-by.

"Ok, where are you?" Worlz thought.

"I'm in the cave at the cliff. Berhpas is gone. I found a wall like the training walls back home. Only, this one is different. You have to come see," Rhom Said.

"You shouldn't be in there. Berhpas may not like it if he finds you there."

"That is why I am reaching out to you. Can you quickly find Cloi and Brawzen? Tell them to enter and guard the room. I need to test something." With that, Rhom turned his attention out beyond the mountain range toward the forest. He shot off like a rocket.

"Wait, Rhom! What happens if you go too far from your body?" Captain Worlz asked.

It was too late. Rhom had moved beyond the captain's range. Rhom made it far enough that he could see the clearings in and around the Havens before he felt himself "thinning." Not enough to get to Yereni, but it was something. The view was amazing and his ability to communicate was tenfold. If only it could have been more, he might have been able to find Yereni and speak to her.

Returning to the camp, the power of the enscribed wall grew. Rhom located Uncle Brawzen and Cloi. The location of their presence was close together. They must already be in the cave. He spoke to both.

"Is the room clear?" Rhom asked.

The shock of hearing his voice in their head was greater for Brawzen than for Cloi. Perhaps the captain had shown her something of his Stranded gift.

"It is for now," Cloi responded.

"What is this?"

Rhom could hear Brawzen's thoughts racing through an onslaught of questions.

"No, I am not dead and no you are not going crazy." Rhom was busily trying to calm the thoughts of the confused Brawzen. "Yes, that is my body, but my mind is behind you. I know it sounds weird. I can explain in a moment."

Reaching out, Rhom connected his mental impression to that of Brawzen, pulling him into the mind pool. At first, Rhom wasn't sure it would work, but the inscriptions resonated with such power it was worth a try. Brawzen was a heavy mind. The weight of maintaining his connection to the vision was taxing Rhom. Holding on a moment longer to allow Brawzen to pan the room, he broke the connection and returned to his own body.

"H-H-How is it possible?" Brawzen sat blinking,

looking at Rhom.

"I am not altogether sure. I know it has to do with the vespridium, but also something more." Rhom was building connections in his mind as he responded. "I have seen a vision of another, a goddess, a mother. It is unclear who 'they' might be. I do know there is another powerful being out there. I heard Terth speak of it as well. I can only believe he has had an encounter with vespridium objects or a powerful location like this one. I wish Berhpas were here to explain it."

"If this power is discovered the Jamtori will pollute it and more innocent lives will be lost. This room is dangerous. We should destroy those markings." Brawzen reached down and grabbed a heavy grapefruit-sized stone to throw at the wall. Cocking his arm back, he put all his weight behind his toss. A firm hand caught him in mid-motion.

Captain Worlz spoke as he continued to hold Brawzen's forearm. "We need to understand the purpose of this power. What if by destroying it, we set loose something worse?"

Relaxing his arm, Uncle Brawzen looked at Rhom, whose face seemed to have aged so much in the past few months, and sighed.

"You are right. If we are to make peace with all Crelli, we must not start with rash actions and quick judgments." Brawzen's words were both redemptive and motivating.

"What about the real reason we are in this room?" Cloi's question brought the group back into focus. "If Berhpas is not here, where is he?"

"I have never been in here before today. It was his habit to meet at the water. The tunnels would take weeks to search, and the people are moved to rescue their fellow

Crellan. A search in here would only bring suspicion and more confusion. Especially that wall over there and the power it contains," Captain Worlz replied.

Rhom said, "I think with some practice I can travel farther. I could just see the Havens on my first try. The mines are farther, but if I link with Worlz, I might hitch a ride, so to speak. It is strange but after I traveled through the wall, I could see a glow around you, Worlz. I also saw something similar around the Citadel. It must be the connection to the vespridium. Perhaps I can find Yereni the same way. If not, I still may discover more about the captives once we are near."

"Cloi, somebody needs to stay and protect Rhom's body," Worlz said. "There isn't anybody in the camp I trust more than you. Brawzen must go to see if Terth is truly the menace and perhaps reason with him. Rhom is going to be here and sort of there, and I will be his tether. Besides the people..."

"You don't have to say anymore," Cloi said. "I know what is required of me. Just make sure you bring them all back, and you return in one piece."

It had been several days since the event in the cave, and the teams were ready. Goodbyes and well-wishes were passed between the volunteers and those remaining at the camp. Every spare harness and mon-ton had been repaired and equipped. Three units were formed. A rag-tag assembly of one hundred and fifty Crelli marched out that day, eager to reach the trees and make their way down to the valley. The plan was to skirt south of the Havens and cross the river near the Vigrop marshes and travel northeast to the cave mouth just inside the border of the Bellopian Sursa.

Scouts were dispatched early that morning, marking the trees as they forged a path. In addition, an emissarial envoy with sealed papers departed later that day. Tasked with returning to the Havens, their goal was to quickly speak to the people directly before the Masari or the Jamtori could intercept them. Once knowledge of the captives was given to the people, it would be difficult for the Citadel to contain the truth.

The disappearance of Berhpas had spread discord among some Separatists, and Worlz used the Emissaries to provide hope to those who longed for peace. It offered a path to going home, home to the Havens. Worlz was also trying to buy time to discover what truly happened to Berhpas.

At that same time, Cloi began exploring the faceted openings inside the cave. Each tunnel was smooth and similar in shape and diameter. She wondered what type of mechanism had been used to forge the pathways. It differed greatly from the tunnels and caverns in the mines. The passages continued deep into the mountain. It could take a long time to map it all out.

While Cloi was exploring the rest of the cave, Rhom spent his time studying the symbols on the wall. He wrote them all down to find any commonalities between the symbols inside the cave and those woven into the lattice on the platform near the water's edge where he had been meeting with Berhpas. He learned that if he prepared his mind and body for the transition of pacing through the portal, he could maintain his focus for about four hours before needing to return to his body. He used these sessions to evaluate the limit to his traveling distance.

The farther he went, the darker and foggier the world seemed. A haze covered the land beyond his sight. Rhom could see the Havens, at least the shadows of its location but could not get close enough to hear any thoughts. He had watched the emissary party leave and would make a "pit-stop" with their thoughts each day. It would take the party four to five days to reach the Havens and the Citadel.

On the third day, Rhom decided to search north of the caverns, beyond the range of rock cliffs. Skimming the peaks, Rhom descended onto a high plateau of trees reminiscent of the tumble trees found just below the Separatist camp. Pressing forward, he entered a large round valley with vegetation that was like home. Rhom could see a ripple in the misty haze just beyond. He knew he was nearing his limit, but something was out there.

Suddenly, he was stuck. Rhom's entire presence was frozen in mid-air. His soul self was trapped.

"Little one, I see you have found the Architrave." The voice was familiar. "I told you before, you are not alone. You are a part of me. I am the Remplancant. I am your mother."

Rhom was afraid. He tried not to think of anything, or at least think of objects he could see. He focused on the water, trees, leaves, clouds, and anything to keep his mind clear and somewhat empty.

"It is no use; I can hear them anyway. Once you pass through the Architrave, you enter my realm. I call you mine because your body possesses a portion of my power. It was not intended for your kind. It is for my first children, the ones you call Visatae. You, little one, are merely an ember of the light which is to come once my children reach their prime. Already others are at work freeing my offspring from their buried prison.

"The other embers have embraced me and even now hunger for more of the catalyst which has opened their eyes. Especially Terth, yes, you know him well. Your thoughts are filled with him and the other—the female. She will be your undoing. Her power is indeed unique. In time, it will consume her, but not before she has devoured many others."

While the Remplancant was speaking, Rhom tried desperately to restrain his thoughts. The ripples created by her presence pounded him rhythmically. Rhom was trying to recover his voice, only he couldn't form any type of strategy without his thoughts being read. But as her words hit home about Terth, his own anger rose. As soon as he heard the Remplancant's decree concerning Yereni's future, Rhom could not contain his own rage.

"NO!"

The anguish of a dozen emotions welled up inside him. The ripples that had been until this point continually slapping into him were repelled by his own outward bubble of energy. The atmosphere crackled around him as his emotions burst forth.

"You seem to say that a lot. Aren't you tired of fighting against the fates? I have chosen you as the voice of the future. You can be the one to bring order to this world. I can show you how to use your voice. With my guidance, it may even be possible to change the course of the girl's destiny. Surrender to me and I can be the one to complete your transformation and make your ember as bright as the stars."

As the Remplancant continued to slather on, the charm of her voice faded into the ugliness of avarice. Rhom realized the wall created by his emotions was concealing his thoughts. He looked for an opening to repel the onslaught. With one last surge of primal emotion, he pushed away from the range of waves. Just free of the web spread by the Remplancant, Rhom could still hear her voice, but the binding power of her presence was gone.

"It matters not where you travel in my realm or the other. I can find you. This is not over little light. The power of my successors grows each day. The Visatae Dobai will soon consume your land. Without me, you will be alone and forsaken. The others will mistrust you because of your ability. It is simply a matter of time. All the Architraves lead to me. I am the gatekeeper, Guardian of the Crepus Caliginous. The Refulgenae are gone and Jaru is with them. What remains is mine and no mere flicker can stand against the power of my light."

Rhom reversed course and returned to the cave out of fear the gateway would be closed. Upon awakening, he found Cloi standing over him, eyes wide as saucers. The wall was still carrying a faint glow across the surface. Rhom leaned forward, placing his head between his knees. His body ached from head to toe. His palms were clammy, and the room felt cold.

"We must hurry. I have seen her, I have seen the Remplancant. We need to find the other Archetraves... Visatae Dobai...Yereni. It is too much." Rhom collapsed forward and fell asleep.

Rhom opened his eyes slowly. Turning as he made his way to stand up, he saw Cloi sleeping on the pile of bedding. Behind him, a plate of food was on the table to her left. Peering through the dimly lit space, he could see he was still in the cave at the rear of the compound. The room was the same as it had been, but he had learned something new. A group called the Refulgenae created the patterns on the wall. The portal he was using was called an Architrave. He wanted to know more. Speaking with the "mother," the Remplancant, was dangerous, but the desire for more knowledge burned in his mind. He knew what he must do.

Instead of pressing into the wall, Rhom let his mind search the symbols, looking for the sequence to activate the portal. Like the Jamtori trials, activating the correct sequence was rewarded with a lingering blue light along the correct symbol.

"You must be tired, Rhom; your glow has gone from blue to green," Cloi said. Rhom was so focused on the wall he didn't even hear her approach.

"What did you say, Cloi?" Rhom replied as he

continued to probe the symbols.

"Your glow," she said. "You know, the light around you. Everyone has it. I can't always see it, but when I do, it helps me know who to trust."

"What does this glow do? How do you know who to trust? Explain this. It is especially important." Rhom was overly excited.

"Well, gold, green, and light blue people are safe. Orange, red, and violet are not always good. There are other colors, but those I can't always pin down." Cloi reached for a piece of fruit as she said this.

"Cloi, have you told Berhpas about this? Is it possible you have been gifted as well? If I focus on the wall, can you tell me what happens to my color?" Rhom was thinking fast. A theory was forming.

"Sure, normally I see blue tones float in and out like waves. Then the color passes through the wall and your body falls."

Rhom placed himself in front of the wall. Digging deep, he dove into the depths of the mind pool. Finding Cloi, he linked with her thoughts. Rhom began reaching out to the symbols around the wall.

As Rhom probed the wall, waves of color flowed from his hand, igniting each symbol as he passed them across the wall. The wrong sequence and the symbols no longer produced an aura. The thoughts projected by Cloi provided vital information about Rhom's choices on which symbol he would activate. The shared process of exploring the wall was working. After many trials the last symbol on the outer ring was fully lit. A pin of blinding white light burst into the room. Next, the two of them tackled the riddle of the inner wheel.

Rhom extended his palm toward the utmost symbol of the wheel. A whomp of pressure pushed him away from the wall as the beam of light in the center grew. The wall faded away. It was as if the rock was sucked into the light. This was not an astral projection. The opening was both physical and energy. Grabbing Cloi by the hand, Rhom dove into the light. For a moment he felt upside down, inside out, and backward. The next moment, the two of them were in a dark room similar to the cavern they just left. There was one difference between this cavern and the other, this cavern had only one tunnel. The two were amazed and bewildered by what had just happened.

"Let's go see where we are," Rhom said as he swung his open palm out as if to say 'you first' to her.

She looked at him, then down the tunnel. "Ok, but whatever happens, just remember it will be your fault, and by the way, when we get home, you owe me a drink." She smiled as she turned to enter the tunnel.

"Wait! I have a better idea. If I can pass through the other one by diving, perhaps I can scout around here too." Rhom sat in front of the carved wall, palms pressed against the cool rock. Relaxing his mind, Rhom dove into the Mist. It was empty, so dark it couldn't even be called black. Black was something, this was nothing. "I must be inside rock," he thought as he willed his body to move left. It was an odd experience to push through the void. Rhom counted to ten and made another left. This time, he counted to five and turned left again. Pushing forward, he could faintly detect the waves coming from Cloi's mind. The interference from the portal was now on the other side of her location.

"I can see your mind echo. I want you to tell me if you can see any aura."

"Rhom, I can see the wheel on the wall."

"Okay, turn around and tell me what is there."

"I see a faint blue, almost white, glow. It is far away

and looks like it has waves passing up and down it."

"Cloi, how long have you been able to see the colors?"

"Since I was small, maybe nine seasons. How do you think I did so well at all those games of chance? I can usually read a bluffer."

"Does anyone else know?"

"Worlz knows, but I don't think he told anyone else. I heard Berhpas once say it was common for ancient Crelli to have pre-cognitive intuition and that the Visatae were merely amplifying our latent abilities. I guess I figured it was normal and at the time I was still trying to blend in after all the jokes about getting lost. Which, by the way, you need to figure out where the shreft we are and what we are doing and do it."

His brain was on fire. Captain Worlz was expending too much energy trying to calm his team down. The idea of going against Vigrop impounders and an upgraded Jambat team meant the anxiety levels were high—higher than anything the captain had trained for.

He opened his pack and removed a thin black collar. A round device was mounted in the center. Worlz engaged the activator on the side and strapped it around his neck. The device pierced his spine similar to the connection a Visatae makes. Berhpas had given this to him when he was young. When his empathic connections first began, it would often lead to unbearable strain and sometimes seizures. The needle fed tiny amounts of a narcotic designed to inhibit his abilities. The Jamtori use a modified version of the same device to regulate the removal of Visatae and prevent separation fever. The mixture kicked in and soon he could focus again.

The captain stood up and silently motioned for his second in command. A young, fresh-faced Crelli with gray hair came forward. He was still wearing boots, even though they were now high in the canopy branches. The standard shades of burgundy and gray, with splashes of orange that covered his woven jumper, did their job of blending in with the forest.

"Well, Shives, it is time to divide the teams. Take three units down to the ground and head north. Place them in groups between the large opening in the cave structure Cloi described and the Bellop border as we discussed. I will give you three hours to set up the rest of our plan before we begin our assault on the entrance. Be sure you keep a close eye on the opening. Once the reels have been set, hold your position until we have crossed the clearing at the cave mouth. By now, Brawzen and his team should be securing the rail system at the far opening near the southern marshes. If they are successful, we can use the carts to shuttle the weak and wounded out and away from the main conflict."

"Understood, don't worry, at sunrise we will be ready."

"I don't like the idea of fighting our own people. It makes the inside of my skin itch just thinking about it. If this unit of rogue Jambat is as treacherous as we have been led to believe, this is going to be a long, dark, and bloody day." Captain Worlz turned and set his face toward the cave. Nothing else needed to be said. Shives momentarily placed his hand on the shoulder of his commander before slipping away into the thick foliage.

Everything was in place. Finally, dawn's first light, the signal all were waiting for. Worlz moved into action. Sliding down the hillside, his team gathered along the edge of the clearing.

Squatting amongst the leafy edge, the captain peered into the dark maw of the cavern. A few lights along the inner wall cast a soft glow behind the stacks of crated supplies and equipment. That's when he saw them, two Vigrop taskmasters, and between, a tall Crelli in full Jambat gear, long wings hung down his back. Worlz could not believe his eyes. It was all true. Even with the inhibitor, he struggled to quell the emotional barrage from his team.

The time had come. Moving in, the strike team made their way to the entrance. He grabbed a heavy set of bolas. "I only have one shot at this," Worlz thought. Shifting the weights in his hand as he prepared his throw, the air became violent. Dirt and forest clutter roughed his exposed skin like sandpaper.

Then a voice called out. "Did you really think a mere constable could surprise us?" It was Terth! "I can see all. You did not think to look up. I am the lord of the sky. I am death from above. I am Visatae Dobai!"

As Terth spoke, his body surged. His entire physique had undergone tremendous growth. It was clear he was amplifying his abilities chemically. It must be the connection to this new variant of Visatae.

Terth's hulking form could have taken on any Bellop challenger. It was clear to Worlz that his opponent was the new dominant predator on Crellantan. Nothing could stop him. Terth shot down from the sky toward Worlz. He spread his arms wide as he drew closer to the ground. Before Worlz could react, he was caught by the forearms in the vice-like grip of Terth's powerful hands.

The cold, sharp electric pain of fractured bone shot up his arm past the shoulders and behind his ears. Worlz heard the zazzing sound of scaled wings as his restrained body was lifted from the ground. The pain was incredible. Worlz could no longer contain his hurt. The strain of balancing the ambient empathic waves, compounded by boiling emotions, was overwhelming. The inhibitor around his neck heated as the vespridium device could no longer regulate his energy. A focused beam of pure empathic force invisible to the regular eye shot forth toward Terth.

The rhythmic thrum of wings paused. Terth's eyes sparked as his grip loosened. Worlz could hear a faint pomf, pomf, pomf from below. Thin shadows passed over their aerial duet. Huge, weighted nets had been cast over the clearing from the forest edge. Shives had executed the plan perfectly. A thin smile passed across the captain's pained face as Terth released his hold.

The fall was close to twenty feet. Captain Worlz and Terth were engulfed in the surrounding nets. Terth struggled to rend his way upward. While the battered Worlz did his best to tuck in tight for the fall. As the pair crashed to the ground, a group of reserves led by Shives drove U-shaped stakes through the edges of the net, securing the catch.

Terth was far from giving up. Centering his mass, he firmly grabbed at several interlocking connections. His greatly increased muscular frame was put to the test. Tearing at the net, he burst forth. Powerful legs propelled him toward the new attackers. In a moment, he was in the thick of the group. A mass of whirling dust and undiscernible bodies circled near the edge of the nets. The battle raged as Terth struggled to clear the area, but the weight of numbers was not in his favor.

A cry of rage rang out from behind him. Terth looked back over his shoulder too late. Captain Worlz crashed down upon the back of the bulging Crelli, driving both of his monsu into the open sides of the Visatae cylinder right above the costa of the wings. Terth screamed in pain, collapsing to the ground. The emotional feedback caused by his action sent Worlz reeling. A voice shrieked out in anger.

"How dare you harm one of my children! I had ignored your miserable splashings in my realm since your light was so small. Now you shall know my anger. You have been branded along with the other."

The captain froze, his mind captive.

"The Visatae are mine. I am the Remplancant. My champion will see that you are no more."

Worlz, pained by injury and held captive by the overwhelming grip on his mind by the Remplancant, could only watch as the muscular form of Terth rose from the fray. Terth roared as he turned left and right to face the on-coming Separatist forces. The damaged wings hung limp. Worlz was fading fast. He could no longer keep his head up. Crashing to his side, eyes welled over from pain and tears, Worlz passed out from the overwhelming emotional stimulus.

Cloi and Rhom made their way down the dark corridor. A soft glow far down the shaft was their goal. Cautiously turning the corner, they knew at once they were inside the mines. The portal shortened the seven-day journey to moments. Extending one of her monsu, Cloi marked the ground in front of the tunnel.

"We need to remember this" she said. Rhom nodded, and the two moved on. They decided to head toward the upper holding cells.

"Cloi, I have an idea. I am going back to the portal. I think I can find Yereni. Without her, all of this means nothing to me."

"Rhom, you must do what you feel is right. If saving this girl means that much, you must try. I think I would do the same in your position, no matter the consequences."

The two stood face to face for a moment, each in their own way urging the other to turn first, though their bodies were motionless. Finally, Cloi reached out and buffed Rhom on the shoulder.

"Go, you three-legged clounter bird, and find that girl. I am going to see what I can do to help the captives.

I can manage a few Vigrop." She tried to conceal her emotions, but the bluff was obvious. Turning away, the pair set upon their journeys.

Rhom returned and set himself on the ground directly in front of the new portal, the Architrave. He now knew the name, but this one was different. The pattern of symbols was jumbled. Rhom closed his eyes and let the energy flow between him and the portal. He intended to mind-dive within the gate. Why not? It was connected to the vespridium as he was. Soon, his consciousness felt pulled to the portal like water down the drain. His other self was through and again inside the cave wall. Once again, he felt a slight panic as though he must breathe, but was able to retreat to his training and adapt.

Rhom recalled the shaft behind him and urged himself to move left and south of the tunnel. What seemed like an hour, but which in reality was only a few minutes, passed, and he could see the glow of others in the mist. Gentle ripples issued forth. Rhom maneuvered around each of the individual mind islands, searching for Yereni. He picked at the thoughts as he passed. Terth was indeed the subject of thought for many of the Vigrop he encountered. He found a mixed bag of hope, fear, and concern emanating from the minds he sampled.

Rhom was growing anxious. The alarm had sounded and the number of minds in his vicinity was reducing rapidly. Surely by now Worlz and his team were engaged in an all-out battle at the large cavern exit. At the same time, Cloi would set captives free while, hopefully, Uncle Brawzen was making headway in his march down the shaft.

Three fronts to repel. The Vigrop would be busy. There should only be a few remaining in the center. Rhom searched frantically for Yereni. He stretched his ability to its limits.

"Impressive. How did you get here so quickly? What has she promised you?" It was the voice of Berhpas. He continued, "How did you like the Architrave? I must admit, I did not think you bold enough to try it."

Berhpas here at the mines? Something was off. He sounded different. Rhom instinctively sucked all his energy in to reduce his temporal footprint. His mind fevered, and the anxiety of losing Yereni again was taking over.

"It is no use. I have seen you. There is no way for you to get past me. I am the architect. The Stranded, the Jambat training, the vespridium, and even the conversion of the Jamtori hybrids are all part of my plan. Yes, yes, I know the Visatae were here with us for generations before me. However, nobody could foresee their true use. I struggled and strived to unlock the steps to complete the chain, but my vision was not clear until I met HER.

"The Remplancant, in her wisdom and glory, ignited the fire and set ablaze the path. There is an architrave on the cliffs on the far side of Lake Culumbi. I found it, and her voice spoke to me. The others did not understand. They called me mad. The Masari and his minions tried to end my progress. But I fooled them. I took the children and destroyed the Lab."

Rhom, upon hearing those words, seethed with rage. His thoughts rang out.

"YOU! You? The teacher? Leader of the rebellion? You killed my family. You killed so many others!"

"And look what you have become—powerful, brave, daring, a uniter of the people, all because of my plan. In time you will thank me, Rhom. But I must warn you, Yereni is not for you. I have seen her power. Her father has shown me. Not to mention the others. Terth and his team... very promising. There is no way you can leave. Even now, the rest of your pitiful troop is failing."

Rhom, in his anger, searched everywhere for the concealed villain's location. There was no way he was going to let this murderer get away unpunished. He sent out waves of thought, but not a glow could be seen. Then, he tried no thoughts at all, waiting for Berhpas to reveal himself. It was Flinter's Folly on an amplified level. All Crellantan was at stake. Suddenly, he had an idea. Rhom sent out his waves as before, but this time he scanned for a place where there were no waves. No bounce back.

Rhom scanned silently and methodically. Finally, he found him. Berhpas was absorbing the fluctuations in the Crepus. Rhom shot to the spot like an arrow—laser focused on the other's mind, guided by an aguish unlike any he had felt before. Was the entire world against him? Rhom felt tiny and small for a moment. His mental projection shrank as he approached the shadow of Berhpas in the mists of the Crepus.

His Body! Rhom realized how foolish he had been. Berhpas was merely stalling so his minions could find Rhom's physical body. Turning, he raced to return to the portal. His energy was failing. Whatever was happening outside was definitely not good.

It was now a race for life. Every second counted. He could see several forms in the distance. The gap was closing. Rhom was almost there.

Gasping for air, Rhom reunited with his body only to find he was bound hand and foot. A tight strap was wrapped around his neck, making breathing difficult. He was slowly running out of air.

"Hello, friend." The tone was dreadful, filled with such malice. Rhom recognized it at once. It was Yereni.

"Have you come to cause more pain and

destruction? You are the reason my mother is dead. Have you come to finish your work and kill me?" Her pain and anger rose with each syllable. Rhom was confused, his head swimming from lack of oxygen.

"Father wants to see you," she said, looking directly into his eyes. Rhom saw nothing in them to bring him hope. His vision blurred as the sparkles of dizziness filled his sight. One last thought "Yereni I-I-I'm sorry" and he was out.

Slowly Rhom stirred and lifted his head. The room was dark, and a gray light washed the walls. Above him, a large circular device swayed slightly from the chains holding it.

"Hello, Rhom, we have guests," Berhpas said. "One you already know, so I will introduce you to the other. This is Bendohl, my resolute assistant. You may have heard of him. He has been very productive during our exile." Rhom looked across to see the two of them seated with Yereni standing behind them, arms crossed, scowling. He attempted to reach out with his mind toward Yereni.

Berhpas proudly spoke, "It is no use. This room is a dampener. An anti-vespri chamber if you like. One can't be too careful when dealing with these things, you know. Clever, don't you think? It occurred to me that if I am going to be the ruler of both Crellan and Lord of the Crepus, I need a place to think without the prying gaze of the Remplancant or any others who may be endowed with vespri."

Rhom now knew why Berhpas appeared to absorb the waves. He was using a dampener to conceal his location. It must be the same knowledge used in creating the inhibitor Captain Worlz wears, he thought.

"If this is to be my end, I think I am at least owed an explanation of why. Why did my family have to die? Why are you against your own people? Who is the Remplancant?" Rhom tried his best to sound in control.

"I owe you nothing. You are my creation to do with as I please." Berhpas looked up for a moment at Yereni. "My dear, would you be so kind as to check on the status of what is happening with Terth and his team?" She nodded and turned to leave, pausing short of the door.

"Yereni, this is not like you. Can't you see they are deceiving you? He wants you to leave because he doesn't want you to know the truth. He claims to be my creator. Wouldn't that mean it was his plan, his fault that Mallahen died?"

"Silence!" Bendohl said as he gave Rhom's left cheek a solid punch.

Rhom looked up through his furrowed brow at Bendohl. Licking the corner of his lip and catching the metallic taste of blood, Rhom said, "Keep proving me right."

"You are in no position to say anything, child. You cannot understand the complexities of what I have accomplished." Berhpas continued, "You and your childish actions are the reason she has suffered." He waved his hand toward Yereni in a contrived manner of false courtesy. "You, Rhom, have wounded her deeply and, therefore, invalidated any statements you may try to express."

"Yereni, you found me, healed me. Think of the time at the outpost. I held nothing back. I shared everything with you. We were hap-." Another blow ended the sentence for Rhom.

"This is pointless. Bendohl, take her from the room. I will talk to him alone." Bendohl moved to escort Yereni from the room. He placed a hand on her shoulder and the other at the elbow to position her toward the door. Yereni was solid as a rock.

"End this now. He deserves to die. A fitting reward for a cowardly betrayer, a false friend who watched as my mother's life ended," she said coldly. The words dug deep into Rhom's heart.

"It is true I was not strong enough to defend you. I was subjected to the horror alongside you. It was you who avenged your mother. It was your power, Yereni, that killed the raiding party. I was not the source." This time Bendohl was too far away to exact corporeal punishment.

"Wrong. It was you who killed them. I heard your voice. I saw the blue flames consume the room. Poppa says I can have this power too. If I kill you, I can take that power and deliver justice for all the Crelli who have suffered like me." Her response ended in a quiver. It infuriated Rhom. What kind of hold did these madmen have? Her thinking was skewed.

Turning to Bendohl, he spoke.

"The truth will become known. When she sees what you have done, her fractured mind will come for you, and I don't think I can stop her. In fact, I may not want to stop her. It may be better for everyone if we all just die here."

"Shut up!" Bendohl said as he slooped for the door, bobbing up and down on his hobbled leg.

"Yereni, look at me. Listen. We are the product of merging two worlds. The boundaries between the two are thinning each day. There is an entity on the other side waiting to be freed and cross over. The vespridium is the key. The more we use it, and convert it for our technology, the weaker her prison becomes."

"I have seen the gift you have been given. There are others like us. Even now, they fight outside these walls to free the Crelli trapped below."

Tears wound their way down his face as Rhom

spoke. Behind Yereni, Bendohl hunched at the door, muttering about his experiments. Berhpas merely sat there with his eyes closed.

"I cannot believe a word you say. I will find the truth for myself." Turning to Berhpas she said, "Show me this portal."

Cloi knew Brawzen and his group were making their way down the rail tunnel from the farther end. Perhaps when the alarm sounded, which it surely would, the remaining guards would be reduced to a manageable number for her to slip past and release as many captives as possible.

Crouching in position behind an outcropping of rocks along the open shaft, she waited. Her joints ached as she sat. A pair of sentries crossed along the main room. She gathered from their conversation that Worlz and his units were taking on the main force. She wanted badly to be at his side, but she also knew her presence would have been a distraction. Soon the loud bong of the alarm bell traveled down the tunnel. Vigrop of all types passed her view. Jumping into rail cars and pumping their way up the shaft, the chaotic mish-mashed crew disappeared in silence, leaving a pair of guards behind.

"Time to move, kid, or we may all end up dead," She told herself as she crept up the shaft toward the holding pens.

Cloi shot across the opening, yelling at the top of

her lungs. Reaching for the closest guard, she grabbed his slave prod. She maneuvered into position behind the opponent, pulling the shaft of the prod tight across his neck.

"You want to breathe again? Give me the combination to the lock" she said with deadly intent. The other guard hissed as he wound his way into the typical Vigrop combat style, a low-coiled crouch. His tail was taut and curled out behind in a slight arc. Her enemy had thrown aside his helmet to improve his field of vision. Uttering a low hiss, he attempted to distract her into losing a defensible position.

"You're running out of time. He will die and then you will be next. Now give me the code." She tightened her grip as she spoke. The trapped Vigrop could do nothing. His shorter and smaller arms could not provide enough leverage to loosen the hold. He slumped.

"SSSSSarrrghhh! Okay, SsssOkay, you win. Don't kill him. I am matesss with his sssisster. I can't have that over my head," The Vigrop made his way toward the gate. Cloi relaxed her grip on the other as his body crumpled to the ground. The first guard looked back over his shoulder.

"Don't worry, he will recover." She said, walking toward him.

"You better hit me on the head, or they will never believe me," The Vigrop said as he opened the doors to the pens. Cloi spun the shaft over her head and crossed his head behind the right eye. It was a glancing blow, enough to leave a mark. A thin line of blood trickled down as the impact dissipated. The Vigrop's eyes widened as he fell to the ground. Cloi's blow was perfectly executed. "They are both going to have some headache when they wake up," she thought. As soon as the doors opened, a mad rush of desperate captives pressed past her, looking for any way to escape. Cloi jumped to the top of the nearest rock pile. "Listen! All of you! Stay together. Make your way to the supply staging tunnel. Help is on the way. Stick to the main line and keep moving up the hill. Leave no Crelli behind. Stay calm and move together." She made her way to the shaft entrance. "Everyone keep moving. Help will be here soon." Finally, the last batch made its way past her.

"You," she said to a broad-shouldered Crelli who looked like he could manage himself. "Make sure nobody falls behind." He nodded in silence as he lifted an older Crelli by the elbow to escort him. She followed them for a little while longer, slowly falling back until she thought they were well on the way. She turned and made her way back to the main cavern.

Returning to the detention gate, she dragged the two guards inside and locked it. "Now, to check on Rhom." She crossed the open cavern heading for the dim corridors on the farther side. She was thankful for her quick thinking about marking the tunnels. Completing the route for the portal, Cloi arrived at the spot, but no Rhom. He was gone.

"Shreft!" she spoke. "What now?" Grabbing the shaft of her borrowed weapon, Cloi hurried back to the start, which was really the end. She had not seen Terth or a single member of his Jambat unit. Her instincts were screaming that it was a trap. She stopped for a second and recovered her breath. Closing her eyes, she attempted to find Rhom. She thought his name, called out, and waited. "Rhom," she tried again. "Rhom." One more time, Cloi thought. Still nothing.

Cloi opened her eyes. She remembered the area where they encountered Delpar and the other Jambat during their escape. She bound through caverns toward the bellows, and hopefully the doors beyond.

Turning left quickly, Cloi entered a rather dark passage. The hallway ended in a single door. The latch work was intricate. A series of long rods penetrated the thick rock of the frame and threshold. In the center of the door, she could see a pattern of holes. It was a combination lock. Cloi needed to insert her fingers into the right holes to trigger the correct latches all at once. She studied the holes carefully for wear marks, dust, scratches anything to indicate which holes to use.

"Well, shreft!"

Plunging her hands into the first series of holes, she heard a click.

"Okay, good guess." Cloi pulled her fingers out and made small marks with the end of one of her monsu.

"Now for the second set." This proved to be more difficult. She made several attempts, only to hear a dull thunk and see the first set of rods reset. She made a unique mark for each failed attempt. Finally, the second series was correct. The door opened with a soft gasp of air.

Rhom had just finished his conversation with Yereni about finding the Remplancant when he noticed movement in the doorway. It was Cloi. The fevered Bendohl cowardly crawled out the door. She gave one side glance toward him and rushed toward Rhom.

"We must hurry! The battle outside has begun, and I am worried about Worlz and the others." She was in a frantic state.

"Cloi, close the door but keep your hand on the lever and do not release it," Rhom said.

Yereni looked at one and then the other. Her eyes became slits armed with focused daggers.

"So, I see! Another female you have tricked into trusting you. You are a coward and a slithering verkas."

Cloi cut her off. "Is this the one, Rhom?" thumbing over her shoulder in Yereni's direction. "The girl you had to come back for. The person you mentioned in your sleep every night all the way across the forest. Seeing her now, I am not so sure you made the right decision."

Yereni's face turned red. Anger, embarrassment, and pride all congealed into a lathery mess of emotions.

Rhom shyly flushed as he awkwardly shuffled his feet. An uncomfortable silence passed. Rhom looked up to speak.

"How did you find us?" Rhom said.

"I traced the hallways until I remembered that area where we first saw Terth." Cloi scanned the room as she spoke.

"Cloi, Berhpas is not who he says he is. He has been working with an otherworldly power to conquer Crellan. This entity called the Remplancant is slowly gaining power and plans to permanently open the portals in order to extend her realm."

"I don't understand." Cloi looked at Rhom, then Berhpas and then over at Yereni.

Berhpas rose and slowly turned to position himself between Rhom and Yereni.

Cloi spoke rapidly. "So many things are in motion. Worlz is in danger and time is running short. "

"The Remplancant is not an issue. I can control her," Berhpas said. "This mess you two idiots have made of my plans can be cleaned up. If something happens to Worlz, that will purely be your fault." Moving closer to the door, Berhpas continued, "Yereni, come with me. I will take you to the portal. Together we can search for the answers you seek. Bendohl was indeed responsible for your upbringing, but it was by my direction. Your mother knew this and only wanted a safe place for her child, away from the prying eyes and greedy grasp of the Masari and his Jamtori. Everything is connected, and the Visatae are the key. The Remplancant is an ancient being who once lived on Crellantan. The Visatae are creatures she either created or manipulated to her desire. She considers them her children."

"When the Visatae hatched, the Remplancant detected their presence. As we experimented with vespridium, the barrier designed to keep her weakened. I used the portals to communicate with the Remplancant and offered to reunite her with her children in exchange for knowledge. In her desire to end her isolation, she shared knowledge with me on how to use and control the vespridium. By containing it in vaults like this room, it reduces the powers of the Remplancant."

Suddenly, the door burst open. A crew of armed Vigrop entered the room. "Lord, the attackerssss are gaining ground. We need your help. Skelkiz requests your orders."

"Seize those two!" Berhpas shouted as he ushered Yereni behind him into the hallway.

The group turned to face off against Cloi and Rhom.

"Well, Rhom? It's your turn for a plan. How do we get out of this one?"

Turning toward the door, Rhom made eye contact with Yereni.

"All I can ask of you is to remember. Think about the days we spent together. The freedom you enjoyed away from everything else. The conversations we had. The laughter. All of it was real. For me, it was the most joy I have ever felt. I want that back. I want our friendship back, Yereni."

Yereni stood there, biting her lower lip. Finally, a spark twinkled in her eye.

Turning to Berhpas, she said "I don't even know you. At least I know he is not friends with the Vigrop and trying to destroy the Crellan." With a quick duck to the left, she came up behind the closest guard, yanking his prod from his hand. That was all the distraction Cloi needed. Soon, the group was out into the corridor in an all-out match. Then Berhpas slipped away. With Berhpas gone, the Vigrop faltered.

Rhom cried out, "Push them back into the room!" The three of them poked and prodded and fought the smaller reptilians back through the opening. With a slam, Rhom shut the door, locking the attackers inside.

"Cloi, can you find your way back to the portal?"

"I left a few marks along the way. It's not like I get lost or anything," she said with a quick wink. The two turned, with a hesitant Yereni in tow, around a couple of corners and on toward the portal. The distance was less than Rhom thought it would be. With the Vigrop fighting on two fronts, the rest of the hallways were empty of trouble.

The three Crelli positioned themselves in front of the portal. Rhom and Cloi propped themselves up back-to-back, knowing their bodies would slump over the moment Rhom passed the portal. Yereni looked at the two of them awkwardly.

"What are you doing?" She asked.

"This is your chance to see for yourself. Are you coming or not?"

"I want to see the Remplancant." Sitting down with a quick slump, Yereni placed a rock between them to keep from leaning on the others. Cloi looked at Rhom, who shrugged in response.

"Ok, for this to work, I am going to have to explain a couple of things. Yereni, think back to when we first met, when you would ask me about what we would do in the Havens as kids. Remember how I told you about the games we played? Flinter's Folly—try to remember." She nodded slowly. "OK, now close your eyes and try not to think about anything. Slow your mind down. Imagine you are lying down in a pool of cool water. No sounds, just your own heart pumping. Feel its rhythmic pulse like waves on the shore of the lake. Your thoughts are like pebbles tossed into the waves. You break the rhythm, and she will find you." Rhom slid his hands across the symbols. He was already connected to Cloi. Plunging into the mind pool, he saw Yereni for the first time. Her light was immense. The Remplancant would see them the instant they crossed over. Especially at this portal with so much vespridium in play, the dimensional boundaries were already blurred.

The trio crossed over. The waves of energy refracting all around. The world was dark. "Come, feel the wave from my thoughts and 'will' your way toward me." Cloi and Yereni slowly drifted to the projection of Rhom. "Now up and out."

Up their forms flew out of the caves and into the sky just above. They could see the chaos in the clearing off to the east. Terth and his assemblage of Jambat hybrids and Vigrop henchmen were deeply entrenched in combat with the Crelli freedom fighters.

"Yereni, this is but the threshold between the two realms. We are still bound to Crellantan. The Remplancant remains bound to the other side, but she is powerful nonetheless."

Cloi spoke out. "I can feel a pressure coming, Rhom. Is it her? The voice?"

A sliver of black light spread before them not like the dark of night or what they would see when closing their eyes. It was more like an energy that absorbed light but was also light but not in a spectrum they could fully discern. The power of the Remplancant was growing.

The staging area at the mouth of the tunnel swirled with the tide of combat. Brawzen and his ragged bunch of mountain volunteers were giving the Vigrop slavers an excellent fight. Cart after cart of fresh troops rumbled up the tunnels to join in defense. Each time, Brawzen rallied his troops to press deeper into the tunnels.

"Push, Crelli. We must keep them from the open areas. If we can fight them in the narrows, they can't use their full force." The invaders split into two groups and drove the Vigrop back down the mouths of the tunnels. Momentum was in their favor as the tired Crelli fought on. That was when he heard it. A low thoom echoed from the darkness. A large Bellop waded his way through the slaver forces. The Vigrop cheered as he approached. "Garthag! Garthag!" They shouted and raised their weapons in exultation.

The beast was enormous. A harness of dark leather crisscrossed his barreled torso. His hands were covered with the standard heavy-plated finger slings. Brawzen could see the Visatae mounted on his back. The wings were too small to carry his bulk aloft, but the propulsion they provided gave his stride additional swiftness.

Brawzen gulped and cinched the straps of his monsu. "By the Axioms of Jaru, this is going to be a mountainous task," he spoke as he grabbed a long pole from a fallen Vigrop. "Clear the way, brethren, I must face this challenger alone."

"This one looks too old and stringy," Garthag rumbled as he took position. "I might have to boil him first before eating." The tunnel shook as he pounded his armored fists into the ground. Grabbing ahold of the track, he ripped up a piece of the rail and hefted it like a club, swinging it back and forth.

Brawzen edged his way around the brute, carefully stepping to keep his balance and maintain a defensive posture. Garthag swung with incredible force, but his opponent was just out of range. As the two warriors maneuvered within the cavern, the fighters from each side grouped at opposite ends of the tunnel. Brawzen was careful not to turn his attention from the amassed party of Vigrop. Weaving side to side, he worked the upper end of the tunnel.

Another swing, but this time the Bellop surged forward using the full speed of his Visatae symbient. Brawzen lowered his stance, raised his left forearm, and cross-supported his bicep with his right just in time to block the makeshift club. A loud clang reverberated down the shaft. The force of the blow drove Brawzen back a good four feet. His forearm stung with the pain of the impact. He looked down to inspect his gear. The outer tube of the monsu housing was crushed, and oily mist spewed from the tube connected to the compressor tank. Moving his hand, he engaged the trigger. The monsu extended halfway, stopping with a screech of metal against metal. Once more, the dangerous steps of this dance for life commenced.

Meanwhile, the team in the other tunnel faced a struggle just as daunting. Two of Terth's original Jambat team, Valden and Craznak, had arrived and were dispatching Crelli with exacting skill. It was unclear whether they acted independently or in conjunction with the Visatae, but the blows were incapacitating. It appeared the goal was to disable the aggressors and replenish the slave stock. The number of unconscious and injured Crelli was proliferating. The Crelli were driven back. Soon they would be out in the open again and the Jambat could use their wings.

"Stop resisting!" Valden stood firmly in the tunnel with Craznak positioned strategically at his side. "The Dobai are the future. We are the successors of the Jamtori. Jaru has forgotten us. There is only the Remplancant and Terth is her champion."

The Crelli invaders were indecisive. A rift in factions swirled through the group. Some wavered and lowered their weapons. The crowd looked around with growing distrust.

A young Crelli shouted from the side of the tunnel.

"Rise, we are not here to decide what gods to believe in. We fight to save the Crelli imprisoned below. Figure out your faith on your deathbed. Now is the time to fight. Now is the time to stand or there will be no Crellan left. Do you not see these two abominations are in league with the Vigrop? Fight on. Fight to save our people."

As he finished his statement, the youth swung a long staff fitted with a spike from a broken monsu above his head and down through the helmet of the closest enemy he could reach.

"So be it," Craznak uttered as he leaped into the crowd.

Renewed energy rolled through both forces, erupting in a crescendo of bodies with Valden and Craznak in the center. Scores of incapacitated Crelli were strewn across the tunnel floor, but the invaders were losing ground. The chance for victory was slipping away.

The Remplancant spoke. "There is no escape. You cannot hide from me. This is my realm. I am the centrifuge. Without me, there is no Vespri and no future for your people. Oh, you think this world would be better without the Visatae? They are the foundation of your species. It is because of the Vespri that evolution occurred. The food I produced for them; the diet forged from light. Ages ago, I formed them before the Refulgent Ones exiled me. My children lay sleeping in the soil to be discovered by your kind. You took the babes and their nourishment for yourselves. It was I who authored the forming of the Strands. I gave them the tools to repurpose their genetics. If I cannot leave this prison, I will bring the Crepus Caliginous to them. The doorways will be open soon and the age of the Remplancant will commence. You are nothing. The smallest of sparks, light so faint and indiscernible. "

"And what will happen to us? The ones who have been infused. The stranded." Rhom was deep in discussion with the Remplancant. The more she spoke, the deeper he probed. The arrogant creature hid nothing from him.

"Your resistance is of no consequence. I have chosen Terth as my champion. He will take his place at my side and this one with you will be his mate."

Rhom felt the link waver between the three of them as those last words were uttered.

He could sense Yereni's thoughts as they formed. Once again, she was the pawn in somebody else's scheme. The rage she manifested intensified. Instense feedback from the anger placed an overwhelming strain on his abilities. Cloi could sense the spikes in Yereni's aura.

"That will not happen as long as I am alive!" Yereni screamed.

Caustic waves of charged thought ensued. "Do not test me!" the Remplancant said with commanding force. The wave of her voice flowed out in one long roll like an ever-expanding bubble. The trio's link was shredded.

Returning to their bodies as swiftly as possible Cloi at once stood up to head for the mouth of the tunnel. She looked over her shoulder to ensure the others were following.

"C'mon, we have to hurry before more get hurt," she called out over her shoulder.

Rhom and Yereni stood in silence, staring at each other. The yawning chasm of unspoken and difficult words was there between them.
Rhom stammered, "Yereni, I..."

"I'm done with everybody," she cut in. "I am done. I am leaving, and this time don't follow me. Don't even try to find me. I will hunt down Bendohl, my `father' and make him pay for this. Never again will I trust another Crellan, and I refuse to be manipulated again." She stood there stiff as stone. Her eyes welled, and she bit her lip. Her teeth were clenched so tight, a small droplet of blood appeared. Cloi reached out and grasped Rhom by the shoulder.

"WE DO THIS NOW! Rhom! We have no time to lose."

Rhom turned to look at Cloi. Her stern look snapped him back into focus. The sound of quick feet could be heard. He looked over his shoulder as the faded silhouette of Yereni disappeared.

Rhom could not help but let out a few tears of his own as they ran. He was so sure once they were in the Crepus, Yereni would have seen the truth and known how much she meant to him and that he was not to blame as she thought. He wanted to embrace her and feel the warm, friendly connection of those first days again. He felt small and severed. The task he'd agreed to execute was going to be hard and if he had Yereni by his side, then it would have been ok. He might even be strong enough, but now he had his doubts.

Rhom sat down in front of the portal once more. He was not seeking to enter the Crepus again, but rather to bypass it and use the Architrave to find Visatae. Resontas was the key. It was difficult to clear his mind as his emotions were strung so high from the swirling events around him. Yereni was at the forefront, along with all of those he knew struggling throughout the compound. He retracted deeper into his mind to happier memories. A small drip sound occurred in his consciousness. Focusing on this sound, the world around shrank until it was a small prick of light, merely a head of a pin. Passing through the plain of conciousness, the light inverted. The pinhead beam grew bigger, and he knew his mind dive was complete.

The slumped form of his body lay there lifeless as he traveled past and up the corridor. He could see Cloi standing guard. She would make sure nothing happened to him while he was "out." Rhom turned left and headed up the shaft toward the cart tunnels. Taking the left one, he zoomed along as fast as he thought he could go. Up ahead, he sensed the conflict raging between Uncle Brawzen and the large Bellop. He sent out his thoughts to alert Brawzen to his intent.

"Uncle, it is me, Rhom." Rhom kept repeating himself as he drew closer. Brawzen was on his back with the towering Bellop above. He could see that Uncle Brawzen's leg was mangled into a horrible shape. His knee was likely broken. Several shattered spear shafts lay about. A long thin slice of open flesh along Garthag's right ribs revealed the brute had lost much blood.

Rhom reached out to the Visatae mounted to Garthag's back and spoke a few words. The utterance was not words in such that they could be phonetically described. It was the language of the Refulgenae. The language of light. The mere execution of the act wrenched Rhom to the core. He felt the energy leave him as it exacted its intent on the Visatae. A cold tingle throbbed through him. The creature instantly emitted a soft blue light. The wings folded down into a resting state. The Bellop too seemed to become drowsy as his stance wavered. Swaying to and fro, the mighty Garthag tumbled face down upon the tunnel floor.

Turning his attention to Uncle Brawzen, Rhom reached out to connect with him once more.

"Uncle, please nod your head if you understand the Visatae are not to be destroyed. I can explain more later, but I need to know you can hear me."

Nodding his head several times, Uncle Brawzen leaned up on his elbow and motioned to the onlooking Crelli. The closest few quickly assumed defensive stances around him. With Garthag down, the amassed group of

Vigrop enslavers looked dismayed. The momentum was clearly shifting in favor of the Crelli.

"Give up now before more of us are hurt or injured. We clearly outnumber you." Brawzen wheezed as he spoke. His face telegraphed the pain he was experiencing despite his best effort to conceal it. "Crellan, guard the body of that sleeping giant, but do not touch him."

Rhom had already turned around to intercept the second group in the parallel tunnel. As he made his way up the shaft, he was having trouble sensing anyone familiar to connect with. This is going to be difficult. How would he explain the process of connecting mentally? He needed to reach out to a trusted source.

Nearing the group, he realized the choice was already made for him. There, in the center of a heap of bodies, stood Valden and Craznak. The strewn about Crelli were, for the most part, unconscious, with a few stragglers nursing a disabling injury. Limbs were dislocated or cleanly broken, but nothing life-threatening. Rhom turned his focus to Valden to determine a motive. This was nothing like the raw thoughts of the Bellop from the other tunnel. Valden believed he was doing the right thing as a Jamtori. He was earnest about his goal of protecting the people, even if it meant locking them up or having them work in the tunnels. His thoughts reflected a long-term goal of Crelli dominion. Something Rhom had heard a lot recently. Perhaps there was hope for the Jamtori, maybe there was a chance Terth could be convinced to alter his course too. Rhom focused on the Visatae connected to the two Jamtori. Again, using the newly found secrets of the Remplancant, Rhom was able to subdue the creatures. In turn the Visatae extended the command to Valden and Craznak whose bodies crumbled to the floor dormant.

"Well done Captain, well done."

Worlz looked up to see Berhpas and an unfamiliar Crelli walking toward him. Terth was unconscious. The Visatae mounted to his back oozed blue trails along his back and onto the dirt beneath. Remnants of shredded netting, broken gear, and injured bodies littered the area. Small pockets of the ending struggles of battle could be seen in the open cavern behind them, but it was clear the Separatists had won the day. Worlz was hunched slightly, body heaving from exhaustion. He had a long gash along his rib cage, curving under his arm. Calling out to his second, he said, "Shives, gather everyone together and set up for tallies in the cave. Be sure to secure the inner entries immediately."

"Good, good," Berhpas spoke with a soothing voice. "I see your inhibitor is damaged. Are you quite sure you can manage with all this feedback? Let's move over away from the group and see if I can fix that. Don't worry about this beast of a Crelli, you, uh, defeated. I will have Bendohl here. Watch over him." Berhpas wrapped his arm over Worlz's shoulder and directed him to the far side of the

clearing, toward the cliff edge. "Now have a seat and let's see what I can do with this." Worlz, exhausted from the recent events, leaned back against the dusty clay cliff wall. Closing his eyes for a brief moment, he was soon asleep.
Inside the cavern, news soon came to the assembled Crelli that the teams in the tunnels were successful. Many of the imprisoned Crelli had been freed and led to safety out the other end of the tunnel system. The remaining Vigrop were detained in the large room, housing the bellows. The rest of the facility was now being searched for other victims.

Disturbing feelings and shadowy images raced through Worlz's dreams. The voice he heard while fighting with Terth winnowed its way into his heart. Small, Branded? Other? Tossing, he awoke with a jolt. Opening his eyes, he was greeted by an armed and sneering Bendohl. Leaning over him. A broken and jagged shaft poised firmly in his hand, ready to strike.

"You have destroyed my creation. I will have your life as payment!" Bendohl shouted as he leaped for Worlz. The shaft in his hand hit home, striking directly above his hip on the right side and passing through, pinning Worlz to the ground.

Without his inhibitor, the extreme pain transformed into intense emotion. Worlz's energy burst forth, sending empathic feedback directly at Bendohl. The amplified pain recipient reeled back in anguish. Stumbling as he recoiled from the unexpected counterattack, Bendohl wavered at the edge of the plateau precipice. Below the exposed cliff wall descended a good fifty feet of dry slope before the tips of the trees shrouded the true depth. Flailing his arms, Bendohl landed and tried his best to keep his balance on his misshapen leg. His good leg ranged out behind him.

It was too much for his physical limitation to

handle. Toppling headfirst, he tumbled down the side of the cliff into the vegetation below. His voice trailed as his body disappeared.

A voice rang out across the clearing. Worlz looked up to see Cloi running full speed toward him. A very exhausted Rhom was trailing behind her. Lifting his head one more time, he mouthed her name before his eyes went dim and the world went gray. The echoes of her voice trailed off, and all was silent.

"So, that is how we got to the caverns so fast." Cloi sat on the edge of the bed. Worlz was propped up under a blanket. His body was covered in bandages. Rhom sat in a chair near the door, his elbows resting on his legs and his hands folded under his chin.

"Rhom discovered how to communicate directly with the Visatae. He 'urged' them to rest. After that, we made sure the captives escaped." Cloi was busy explaining everything that happened to them. "Berhpas is missing again but now we know he was working behind the scenes. We have guards set up at both ends of the portal."

"Who was it that attacked me? Why did he do it?" Worlz asked.

"That was Bendohl. It seems he was a subordinate of Berhpas and was involved in creating a hybrid form of Crelli/Visatae soldier. Rhom believes Terth is the prototype. Once you were secured, we looked for him, but the body was gone. Shives and Brawzen think he was taken by Berhpas. The Separatist camp is closing down. We got word the emissaries from the Havens have returned, and the Masari has agreed to meet with us to discuss what has happened. All Jamtori have been recalled to the Havens. I believe the Masari fears a civil war will erupt. Once you have recovered, we will begin the process of incorporation. Many of the captives have already been reunited with their loved ones and are spreading the word about what happened. If the Masari denies the truth too long, he will be seen as an accomplice. The era of the Jamtori rule is coming to an end. The Visatae will be returned to the Remplancant, and the Architraves destroyed."

"It is the only way to ensure peace with the Remplancant," Rhom Said "We cannot afford to have a breach. The opening in the moutain caverns has been destroyed but I do not know how many more there are.

"I will continue to use the portal here at the mines to send the Visatae eggs away." Rhom shifted in his seat as he spoke. "I still want to find a way to save Terth and Yereni. I only hope by offering her children to the Remplancant I can discover a solution. Also, there is the question of what will happen to us.

The vespridium used in our culture is now interwoven into me, you, and countless others who have had prolonged contact. Once depleted, we may find the consequences dire."

Worlz asked, "How is vespridium disappearing a problem? Wasn't that the goal of the movement? Didn't we gather to reject the use of Visatae and the corrupt lifestyle the Masari set up? I thought we wanted to return to the true teachings of Jaru. Berhpas spoke of this often."

Cloi replied, "I asked the same questions. It wasn't until we got back here and started digging into the chambers in the cave that Rhom and I discovered Berhpas had infused vespridium into our water source.

Rhom checked the water back at the Separatist camp. The dais and adjoining areas near the pond and his own living area were designed to distribute vespridium to all of us. He was using the entire camp as a giant experiment."

Just then, Brawzen entered. Hobbling with measured steps, he approached the trio. Bandages and splints covered half his body.

"I, of course, couldn't help but overhear you talking about the future of the Crelli."

"I think it is time we let the Crellan decide what the future will be. Once we return to the Havens and have assembled, we will know what the next move is. Rhom, I for one want you to be there by my side as we give our statements to the council in an open forum for all to hear. It pains me I could not see Terth, but I have hope that a future day will come."

A stern faced Crelli healer walked in. "We need to give the wounded all the time we can to heal before we head to the Havens," the healer said. "It has only been a few days since the battle. There is no guarantee the Vigrop won't return in greater number."

"Ok, ok. Worlz get better so we can get out of here," Cloi said. "Rhom, I think you owe me and the old man here a round at the commissary for all the trouble you have caused running away, getting captured, falling in love with the wrong kind of girl..."

"Wrong kind of girl!" Rhom said. "Now wait a minute. Yereni is out there. I still have a chance. She will come back to her senses, I know it."

"You better toughen up in the meantime, dreamer. Now get moving." Cloi's voice trailed off down the hall. A shadow crossed the window as a hooded figure silently traversed the roofline and descended a low branch into the leafy clumps. Peeling back her hood, Yereni adjusted her gear before descending to the outer wall of the camp.

"Flinter's Folly—hmph," she thought. "I will find Bendohl and balance the scales. Justice will be served by my hand and then I can come back for him." She opened her palm. A small blue light flickered. Slowly, it grew until a small ball of crackling energy hovered above her hand. Closing her fist quickly, the light went out, and she slid away into the darkness.

EPILOGUE

Tall double doors opened in the immense hall of the Bellop Sursa.

The hinges groaned under the immense weight. Long shadows formed along the floor as three cloaked figures entered the hall. The assembled crowd hissed and jeered as they crossed the room toward the elevated platform. The center figure bowed low before the Sursa.

"It is an honor to see you, my Sursa. I am pleased to announce the trials have begun and soon there will be a new soldier to command. My associates and I have successfully merged Bellop and Visatae. The Bellopian Dobai will be ready to deploy by the end of this season."

An enormous hulk of a Bellop looked up from a half-eaten carcass. Tearing a sizeable chunk off, he pointed.

"If I am not pleased with your results, you'll become my next meal," he bellowed out.

The gathered audience whooped out in laughter and raucous howls.

"I guarantee the results will be pleasing." The

speaker raised his hand high above his head. The figures on either side dropped their shrouds and sprung into the air. On his left, winged and armored Skelkiz. To the right, the thickly muscled body of Terth hovered. His eyes glowed blue. Ripples of static energy rolled over his skin. As he lowered his hand, the two minions darted straight for the Sursa.

Berhpas crossed his arms and smiled.

www.ingramcontent.com/pod-product-compliance
Lightning Source LLC
Chambersburg PA
CBHW072108170626
46813CB00004B/1485